Destined Acr

Chapter 1

Caleb Aron Stozick is a mysterious and enigmatic man from the Ethereon galaxy. He hails from a beautiful planet called Cerulea. His race of people are called Luminari. He stands at 6-ft tall with a commanding presence. His straight, shoulder-length hair is a striking dark burgundy color, adding to his otherworldly allure. He bears a rugged, slightly unkempt, appearance, with an unshaven stubble around his mouth that hints at a life of adventure and solitude. The power he possesses goes beyond human comprehension, granting him abilities that defy the laws of nature, which sets him apart from humanity.

Despite his alien origin, there is a sense of longing and vulnerability in his deep, intense gaze, as if he is searching for something or someone on Earth that holds the key to his heart. As he navigates the complexities of human emotions and relationships in his quest to find his soulmate, he must confront his own demons and navigate the challenges of love across the galaxies.

The luxurious spacecraft touched down in a deserted field, surrounded by the lush greenery and rolling hills of Italy. With an air of caution, Caleb activates the invisibility cloak, ensuring that he and his spacecraft remain hidden from prying eyes as he ventures out into the unfamiliar terrain. The quiet beauty of the Italian countryside enveloped him, the soft whispers of the wind carrying a sense of ancient history and untold stories.

Taking a moment to gather his thoughts, Caleb closes his eyes and focuses his mind on his destination. With a subtle shimmer in the air, he employs his teleportation abilities, feeling the familiar sensation of displacement as he is whisked away in a flash of light.

In an instant, he found himself standing on the edge of the Grand Canal in Venice, the majestic architecture and gondolas gliding gracefully along the waterway. The bustling energy of the city washed over him, a stark contrast to the solitude of the deserted field he had just left behind.

Hidden beneath a cloak of invisibility, he navigated the narrow streets and winding alleys, his keen eyes scanning the crowds for any sign of the one destined to be his. As he embarked on his quest to find love and eternal companionship in this foreign land, Caleb knew that his journey was only just beginning. With his extraordinary powers and mysterious presence, he was prepared to face whatever challenges lay ahead in his conquest for true companionship and understanding on Earth.

Caleb took a deep breath and decided to deactivate the invisibility cloak, allowing his true form to be visible to the world around him. With a subtle command, the cloak shimmered and dissipated, revealing his enigmatic presence to the bustling streets of Venice.

As he stepped out into the sunlight, the warmth of the Italian sun caressed his skin, casting a golden glow on his burgundy hair and adding a touch of ethereal beauty to his rugged features. Despite his alien origins, he made a conscious effort to blend in with the vibrant tapestry of human life unfolding around him.

Walking along the cobblestone streets and mingling with crowds, Caleb observed the intricate dance of life in Venice. The chatter of tourists, the aroma of fresh pastries, and the sound of gondoliers singing in the distance created a symphony of sights and sounds that enveloped him in the rich collage of human experience.

With each passing moment, he felt a sense of longing stirring within him, a yearning to find the one who would complete him and understand the depths of his arcane soul. He sensed she was somewhere here in Venice, he just had to find her. As he made his way through the intricate alleyways and picturesque canals of Venice, Caleb embraced the challenges and possibilities that lay ahead in his quest.

As the weeks passed by in a blur of sights, sounds, and experiences, Caleb had explored every corner of Venice, from the crowded marketplace to the quiet, secluded alleyways. Despite his efforts, he hadn't found what he was looking for. Caleb thought that maybe his senses were off in this foreign land, but then again, it was such a strong feeling. He had to keep looking.

One day, he was strolling through an Italian marketplace, the scent of fresh produce filled the air, and the lively chatter of vendors and customers surrounded him. He scanned the crowd, searching for a familiar energy that he knew would resonate with his own. As the day wore on, the feeling that she was near was so strong. Caleb scanned the over the vibrant marketplace, his eyes sweeping over the crowd.

And then Caleb saw her!

There she was, standing at a fruit stall, her fingers gently selecting the ripest fruits with an ease of familiarity that was captivating. The sunlight caught her hair, making it glow like a halo, and he could see the soft curve of her smile as she interacted with the vendor. She was more beautiful than he had ever imagined, and she was his.

Something about her struck him profoundly, like a melody that resonates deep within your soul. A wave of recognition washed over him, a feeling so strong and undeniable that he knew, in that moment, he had found his eternal companion. His journey across galaxies, his search through the vast expanse of the universe, had led him to this moment.

Despite the noise and the crowd, everything around him seemed to fade away, leaving only her in sharp focus. As he watched her from afar, he knew that his journey was far from over, it was the beginning of a challenge that he knew wasn't going to be an easy one. Especially when the subject came up of where he was from, but he was more than ready to meet that challenge head on.

Chapter 2

Meghan Sarah Bedford is a woman of captivating beauty and strength from a small town in South Dakota. Lemmon, South Dakota, known for its wide, open spaces, rolling prairies, and beautiful sunsets. Meghan has a love for open spaces and an appreciation for life's simple pleasures. Her home is a charming, rustic house with a wrap-around porch that offers panoramic views of the surrounding countryside. It is a place where she can spend countless hours of watching the sunset paint the sky with hues of orange, pink, and purple.

Meghan stands out in the crowd with her indigenous Sioux heritage shining in her features. Her shoulder-length black hair, as dark and glassy as a raven's wing, often catching the sunlight and giving off a subtle sheen. Her eyes, instilled with profound depth, mirror her rich heritage and hold an insatiable thirst for adventure and knowledge.

Her 5-ft 9-in tall, slender, yet curvy, body is a testament to her balanced lifestyle. She carries herself with an inherent grace and poise, a harmonious blend of strength and femininity. Her attire, typically a blend of comfortable, yet stylish pieces, complements her figure and allows her the ease to explore to her heart's content.

Being on vacation in Venice, Italy, there's an air of relaxed curiosity and happiness around her as she explores the city's winding waterways and bustling marketplaces. Despite the crowd, Meghan stands out, her aura radiating positivity and warmth.

Unbeknownst to her, her presence has caught the attention of a certain visitor from the Ethereon galaxy, marking the beginning of a love story written in the stars.

Caleb found a powerful pull towards Meghan. His heart pounded as he resolved to make contact, his usual calm demeanor giving way to nervous anticipation. With a determined stride, he walks towards her, his eyes fixated on the graceful woman standing at the fruit stall. As he neared her, he feigned distraction, gently bumping into her amidst the bustling marketplace.

A soft gasp escaped her lips, and a few fruits she was holding tumbled onto the cobblestone. "I'm so sorry," he started, his deep voice carrying a smooth, soothing rhythm that blended with the lively ambience. He bent down to help pick up the fallen fruits, apologizing again. His concern was genuine, and his eyes reflected it.

As he straightened up and their eyes met, he saw her gasp silently. A compliment to his rugged handsomeness? He wasn't sure, but he saw a flicker of something in her eyes, surprise, curiosity, or maybe something more.

"Are you okay?" he asked, his gaze softening. His deep resonant voice seemed to echo around them, cutting through the marketplace chatter.

In response, Meghan merely nodded, still slightly taken aback by the unexpected encounter. Taking this as a cue, Caleb extended his hand, "I'm Caleb," he said, introducing himself, his voice filled with warmth and sincerity. He couldn't help but notice how her eyes lit up at his introduction, a moment that signaled the start of a journey neither of them could have anticipated.

Meghan hesitated for a moment, still surprised by their encounter, but as he introduced himself, something about his warm and sincere demeanor seemed to put her at ease. Gathering herself, she extended her own hand toward his. Their hands met in a firm shake, a simple gesture that held a promise of something more profound.

"I'm Meghan," she said, her voice carrying a soft melody that seemed to blend perfectly with the lively hum of the marketplace. "It's nice to meet you, Caleb." Her words, simple yet sincere, brought a smile to his face. The initial awkwardness of their encounter seemed to fade away, replaced by a growing sense of connection.

As they stood there amidst the hustle and bustle of the Italian marketplace, a unique bond began to form. Gathering his courage, Caleb looked at Meghan, his eyes reflecting a hint of nervous anticipation, "Would it be too bold of me to ask you to dinner?" he asked, his voice steady despite the pounding of his heart. Meghan's face lit up with a smile at his invitation, a spark of surprise and delight flickering in her eyes. "I would love to, Caleb," she responds, her voice filled with warmth.

As she began to give Caleb the address of the hotel where she was staying, a thought entered her mind, did she just agree to have dinner with a man she had just met moments ago? The thought sent a thrill of nervousness and excitement through her. She tried to maintain her composure, but her heart was pounding just as hard as his.

She finished giving him the address and, looking up, locked eyes with Caleb again. There was a moment of silence, a mutual understanding of the unexpected turn their day had taken. As Meghan tried to hide her mixture of emotions, Caleb simply smiled, his eyes reflecting his own anticipation and excitement for the evening ahead. Their chance encounter at the Italian marketplace had evolved into a planned dinner together, a prospect that filled them both with a sense of curiosity about what was to come.

"May I pick you up at seven o'clock?" Caleb asked as his eyes met Meghan's. His voice carried a gentle respect, his gaze never wavering from hers. "That's perfect," Meghan replies, her smile radiant. Meghan felt a rush of excitement, but also a sense of contentment. This unexpected encounter was turning out to be one of the most thrilling experiences of her vacation.

As Caleb prepared to take his leave, he took Meghan's hand with a gentle grip. Bowing slightly, he brought her hand to his lips, lightly planting a kiss on her knuckles. It was an old-fashioned gesture, but it felt right. With that, he met her gaze one more time, a silent promise in his eyes that he would see her at seven o'clock, and they both knew that it would be a night to remember. Bidding her farewell, he turned and walked away, leaving Meghan standing in the bustling marketplace, her heart fluttering with anticipation of the night to come.

After her unexpected encounter with Caleb, Meghan made her way back to her hotel suite, her mind buzzing with thoughts of the evening ahead. As she stepped into her room, she couldn't help but wonder what she should wear. She wanted to look her best, but also feel comfortable. After much deliberation, she finally decided on a short, sleeveless, black evening dress. The dress was elegant and sophisticated, fitting her like a glove and flattering her curvy figure. To complete the look, she opted for a pair of black, semi-high heels, adding a touch of glamour to her outfit. As Meghan looked at herself in the mirror, she felt a sense of eagerness. She was ready for her dinner date with Caleb.

Meanwhile, Caleb arrived promptly at seven o'clock. He stepped out of a luxurious limo, his figure silhouetted against the evening light. Dressed in a dark suit that accentuated his tall, commanding presence, his powerful and imposing figure immediately drew everyone's gaze. As he made his way to the hotel entrance, he couldn't help but feel a flutter of excitement. The evening was just beginning, and he was eager to see where it would lead.

When Caleb entered the hotel lobby, his eyes were immediately drawn to the elevator doors. A soft chime echoed through the room, and the doors slid open to reveal Meghan. She stepped out of the elevator, her black dress hugging her figure perfectly, her heels clicking against the marble floor.

For a moment, time seemed to slow as she moved gracefully across the lobby towards him. The soft lighting of the hotel lobby highlighted the radiant glow of her skin, and her dark hair fell over her shoulders like a waterfall of silk. Caleb could only stand and admire her elegance and beauty. He felt a sense of awe and excitement, knowing that the evening ahead held a promise of a wonderful time.

As Meghan approached him, he offered her a warm smile, and extended his arm towards her, offering her a gentlemanly gesture. "Thank you," Meghan said, her voice soft but steady. She placed her hand on his arm, her touch light but firm. The simple contact sent a thrill up his spine, a sensation he welcomed. With Meghan on his arm, Caleb led her out of the hotel lobby. As they moved in perfect harmony, their connection was palpable, adding an air of intimacy to their every interaction.

Outside, the limo waited, the driver standing by the door. As they approached, the driver opened the door for them. Caleb assisted Meghan into the limo before sliding in beside her, the thrill of the evening making his heart race. As the limo pulled away from the hotel, Meghan couldn't believe that Caleb actually showed up in a limo to pick her up, "This is very nice!", she said, excitement in her voice. Caleb smiled, "Only the best for such beauty."

As they neared their destination, the lights of Alguibagio restaurant came into view. The restaurant, nestled by the water's edge, was renowned for its exquisite Italian cuisine and romantic ambiance. Caleb watched as Meghan's eyes lit up at the sight of the restaurant, her excitement adding to his own. The limo pulled up to the entrance, and the driver opened the door for them. Caleb stepped out first, turning to offer his hand to Meghan.

As they stepped into the restaurant, they were welcomed by the warm glow of the lights and the soft hum of conversation. The charming interior, coupled with the breathtaking view of the water, set the perfect stage for their date. Caleb couldn't help but feel a sense of satisfaction at Meghan's delighted smile, knowing that the night was off to a great start.

Walking up to the host, Caleb confidently stated, "We have a reservation under the name Caleb Stozick." The host, a friendly man with a welcoming smile, nodded and led them through the restaurant. They passed by various tables filled with patrons enjoying their meals, the air filled with the tempting aroma of Italian cuisine. Soon, they arrive at a very private table, tucked away from the crowd. It was an intimate spot, perfect for their dinner date.

The table was beautifully set, with a stunning view of the water outside. As they took their seats, Caleb pulled out a chair for Meghan, helping her to get seated. As she thanked him, he couldn't help but notice the sparkle in her eyes, a reflection of the beautiful evening unfolding around them.

Once they were both seated at the table, the waiter approached them. He was carrying a wine list, which he handed to Caleb. "Le piacerebbe qualche vino in particolare, Signore?" he asked, his professional demeanor matching the restaurant's elegant atmosphere.

Caleb glanced over the list, then turned to Meghan, "Do you have any preferences?" he asked, wanting to ensure she was happy with whatever he chose. "I'm good with whatever you choose," Meghan replied, her trust in his choice evident in her voice. With Meghan's approval, Caleb turned back to the waiter, "Prenderemo una bottiglia di Amarone della Valpolicella," he said, picking out a robust red wine from the Veneto region. It was a fine choice, perfect for a romantic dinner. The waiter nodded and went to fetch their wine.

Meanwhile, Caleb turned back to Meghan, his eyes meeting hers. The candlelight flickered in her eyes, giving them an irresistible sparkle. Breaking the silence, Caleb smiled warmly and said, "Thank you for having dinner with me tonight." His voice was sincere, the gratitude in his tone unmistakable. His words brought a smile to Meghan's face. The sincerity in his voice, the warmth in his eyes, everything about him was genuine and charming. Meghan's smile widened as she met Caleb's gaze. "I'm glad I did, thank you for inviting me," she replied, her voice soft but filled with warmth and sincerity.

In that moment, as they sat across from each other in the romantic ambiance of the restaurant, a sense of connection blossomed between them. It was a connection that went beyond mere attraction, it was a meeting of two souls who had always been meant to find each other.

As they waited for their wine to arrive, the air around them seemed charged with a sense of possibility. The waiter returned with their wine and asked, "Cosa desidera mangiare, Signore?" Caleb replies, "Prendero il vitello e gli asparagi Verdi." The waiter nods, then asks, "E per la Signora?" Meghan tells Caleb that he can order for her. Caleb smiles and tells the waiter, "Lei prendera il Faraona alla Buranea." The waiter nods, "Molto bene, Signore!"

When the waiter disappears, Meghan says, "Thank you, Caleb. My Italian is definitely not as good as yours!" "My pleasure, Meghan," Caleb replies, smiling at her.

After their dinner arrived and the aroma of the delicious cuisine filled the air around them, Caleb decided to add an extra touch of charm to their date. He raised his glass, a playful twinkle in his eyes as he spoke fluent Italian, "Un brindisi alla tua bellezza." Seeing Meghan's puzzled smile, he quickly translated with a warm grin, "A toast to your beauty."

Meghan's eyes lit up with delight at his words. A soft blush colored her cheeks as she raised her glass to meet his, the clinking sound echoing softly in the cozy ambiance of the restaurant. "To my beauty," she echoed in English, her voice soft yet filled with warmth. She took a sip from her glass, savoring the rich taste of the wine.

Caleb couldn't help but marvel at her. Her outer beauty was undeniable, but it was her inner grace, her warmth, and her genuine spirit that truly captivated him. The remainder of the evening was filled with good food, shared laughter, intimate conversations, and a connection that deepened with each passing moment. It was an evening that Caleb would always remember, an evening spent with a woman whose beauty transcended all boundaries.

As the plates were cleared away, Caleb turned to Meghan with a smile, "So, Meghan, is there anything special you would like to do?" he asked, his eyes reflecting a genuine interest in spending more time with her. Meghan thought for a moment, considering the options, she looked out at the twinkling lights reflecting on the water outside, "How about a walk along the waterfront?" she suggested, her voice tinged with excitement.

Caleb's eyes lit up at the idea. "That sounds perfect," he replied, his voice filled with enthusiasm. Standing up from the table, he offers his hand to Meghan, ready to embark on the next part of their evening together. With a smile, Meghan places her hand in his, the connection between them sparking with a sense of adventure and anticipation. As they walked side by side, Meghan couldn't shake the feeling that she had known Caleb forever, knowing full well that she had never met him before today. There was a sense of familiarity and comfort between them, as if they were old friends catching up after years apart. His presence by her side felt natural and right, igniting a warmth in her heart that she couldn't ignore.

Caleb, too, felt a deep connection with Meghan as they walked together. Her easy laughter, her genuine smile, and the way she looked at him with those sparkling eyes, all made him feel like he had found someone special in her.

Caleb turned to Meghan with a curious gleam in his eyes, "So, what brings you to beautiful Italy?" he asked, genuinely interested in learning more about her. Meghan's face lit up with a smile as she thought about her answer. "I've always been fascinated by the history, art, and culture of Italy," she began. "So, I decided to take a solo trip to explore the different cities and immerse myself in the beauty of this country."

She went on to describe her adventures and the places she had visited so far, her eyes lighting up with excitement as she recounted her experiences. Caleb listened attentively, captivated by her stories and the passion with which she spoke about her travels.

As they continued their walk, the world around them faded into the background, leaving only the two of them, lost in the moment and each other's company.

Caleb turned to say something to Meghan at the exact moment she turned to say something to him. Their eyes met, and shared understanding passed between them. Realizing the coincidence, they both burst into laughter, the sound echoing softly in the night air. It was a moment of pure joy, a shared moment of light-heartedness that only deepened the bond between them.

Their laughter subsided, but the warmth of the moment lingered between them. Caleb's footsteps slowed as he turned to face Meghan, the soft glow of the city lights casting a warm aura around them. His gaze met hers with a mix of sincerity and anticipation. With a light pause, Caleb's voice was gentle as he spoke, "Meghan, would it be too bold of me to kiss you?"

Meghan felt her heart skip a beat at his words, her breath catching in her throat. The question hung in the air, laden with unspoken emotions and a promise of something more. She met his gaze, her eyes reflecting a mix of surprise and a flicker of desire. In that moment, time seemed to stand still as they stood face to face, the world around them fading away. The air was charged with tension, the moment hanging in the balance as they both awaited her response. The waterfront was silent around them, the only sound the soft lapping of the water against the shore.

Meghan's heart raced as she considered his question, the connection between them palpable. After a moment, a smile tugged at the corners of her lips, and she softly whispered, "No, it wouldn't be too bold." In that moment, as Meghan's response hung in the air, Caleb felt his heart race with anticipation. The connection between them was undeniable. With a gentle touch, he cups her face in his hands, his touch tender and filled with a mix of longing and affection.

Closing the gap between them, Caleb leaned in slowly, his lips meeting hers in a gentle, tender kiss. Time seemed to stand still as their lips touched, and the world around them fading away as they lost themselves in the moment. The kiss was soft and sweet, filled with unspoken emotions and the promise of something more. It was a moment of pure connection, a shared intimacy that deepened the bond between them.

As they pulled away, their eyes met once more, a silent understanding passing between them. The night seemed to shimmer with newfound magic, the moment they had shared, etching itself into their memories as a turning point in their lives. In that moment, as they stood by the waterfront, their hearts beating as one. Caleb and Meghan knew that this night was just the beginning of something beautiful, a journey of love that they were both eager to embark upon together.

As Caleb and Meghan walked hand in hand back to the awaiting limo, the night air was filled with a sense of contentment and joy. Meghan's smile was radiant, her eyes reflecting the happiness she felt from the magical evening they had shared.

As they settled into the plush seats of the limo, Caleb couldn't help but notice the slight shift in Meghan's demeanor when she mentioned needing to get back to her hotel suite. Concerned, he gently asked, "Is everything okay?" Meghan turned to him, her hand finding his in a reassuring gesture, "Oh yes, everything is more than okay," she replied with a soft smile. "Thank you for a wonderful evening."

Caleb's heart swelled with gratitude and relief at her words. He couldn't help but feel a surge of warmth at the connection they had forged in such a short time. With a glint of hope in his eyes, he asked, "Can I take you to breakfast in the morning?" Meghan's face lit up with a smile as she met his gaze. "I would love to have breakfast with you tomorrow," she replied, her voice filled with genuine enthusiasm and warmth.

As the limo glided through the city streets, the anticipation of the next morning's breakfast date filled the air with a sense of excitement and possibility. For Caleb and Meghan, the night may have come to an end, but the promise of a new day together was about to begin.

As Meghan entered her hotel suite after the magical evening she had shared with Caleb, a whirlwind of emotions swirled within her. She kicked off her shoes and fell back onto the plush bed, the soft comfort enveloping her as she let out a contented sigh.

"I can't believe what happened tonight!" Meghan whispered to herself, her voice filled with a mix of disbelief and joy. The memory of their shared laughter, the intimate connection they had forged, and the sweet kiss they had shared lingered in her mind, each moment etched into her memory like a precious gem.

The room was filled with a soft, warm glow from the city lights outside, casting a serene ambiance that matched the peace she felt within her heart. Thoughts of Caleb filled her mind, his smile, his touch, and the way he had made her feel so cherished throughout the evening. As she lay there, basking in the afterglow of their night together, Meghan felt a sense of gratitude for the unexpected turn of events that had brought them into each other's lives. She knew that this night was just the beginning of something special, a journey of love and connection that she eagerly looked forward to exploring with Caleb.

Caleb asked the limo driver to drop him off just a short distance away. As he watched the limo drive away, he stood alone on the quiet street, a smile playing on his lips. With a flicker of concentration, he closed his eyes and focused his mind, tapping into the power within him. In an instant, he felt his body dissolve into a shimmering energy, and with a burst of light, he teleported himself back to his spacecraft.

Once inside the familiar surroundings of his spacecraft, Caleb's thoughts were consumed by the evening he had just shared with Meghan. The memory of her laughter, her warmth, and the connection they had forged filled him with a sense of wonder and contentment.

"I never expected an earthling to have so much beauty inside and out," Caleb mused to himself, his voice filled with admiration and awe. The image of Meghan's smile, the sparkle in her eyes, and the kindness in her heart lingered in his mind, a testament to the special bond they had formed in just one evening. In that moment, as he sat alone in his spacecraft, Caleb knew with certainly that he had found the perfect woman in Meghan. The connection they shared transcended worlds and boundaries, a rare and precious gift that he cherished with all his heart.

As he pondered the possibilities that lay ahead, Caleb felt a sense of gratitude for the turn of events that had brought them together, and he knew that their journey was just beginning.

Chapter 3

As dawn broke, painting the sky with hues of gold, Caleb found himself wide awake. Filled with anticipation for his breakfast date with Meghan, he decided to find a small café within walking distance of the hotel where she was staying. Drawing on his unique abilities, Caleb focused his energies on teleporting himself from his spacecraft to just a few feet away from the hotel. With a subtle shift in the air around him, he disappeared from his spacecraft and reappeared on the quiet city streets. The cool early morning air was a refreshing contrast to the controlled environment of his spacecraft.

After taking a moment to orient himself, he set off in search of the perfect breakfast spot. The city was just beginning to stir, the soft morning light casting long shadows on the streets. Soon, Caleb discovered a charming little café tucked away in a side street. The inviting aroma of fresh coffee and baked goods filled the air, drawing him inside. The café was quaint, with a small outdoor seating area adorned with colorful flowers and plants. It had a warm and cozy ambiance that he knew Meghan would enjoy.

After discovering the charming little café, the aroma of fresh coffee and baked goods still lingering in his senses, Caleb made his way back to the hotel where Meghan was staying. He walked into the grand lobby of the hotel, the hustle and bustle around him a stark contrast to the quiet of the early morning streets. Approaching the reception desk, he greeted the hotel clerk with a friendly smile.

"Good morning," he said, "Could you please page Meghan Bedford's room and tell her that Caleb is waiting for her in the lobby?". The hotel clerk nodded and promptly carried out Caleb's request. As Caleb waited, he felt a sense of excitement. He was looking forward to their breakfast date and the opportunity to spend more time with Meghan, continuing to explore the undeniable connection between them.

The elevator doors slid open with a soft whoosh and Meghan stepped out. Her eyes immediately found Caleb waiting patiently in the grand lobby of the hotel. His presence was comforting, a familiar face in the midst of the bustling city.

Caleb looked up as she approached, his eyes lighting up at the sight of her. "Ready to go?", he asked, his voice filled with anticipation. Meghan's response was a radiant smile that reached her eyes, transforming her face into a picture of happiness. She nodded, her excitement for their breakfast date evident. "Yes," she affirmed, her voice filled with a warmth that matched her smile.

With her affirmation, they set off together, leaving the grandeur of the hotel behind and stepping out into the city, ready to take on another day of getting to know each other better. As Caleb began to speak, describing the quaint little café he had discovered earlier, Meghan reached out for his hand. Her fingers brushed against his, a soft tentative gesture before she interlaced her fingers with his. The contact was gentle but firm, an unspoken sign of the growing connection between them.

Caleb's words flowed effortlessly as he painted a vivid picture of the café, from the intoxicating aroma of fresh coffee to the charming flowers that adorned the outdoor seating area. His hand instinctively tightened around Meghan's, a subtle acknowledgement of her touch. The morning was off to a promising start, and they both looked forward to the moments yet to be shared over breakfast.

After a pleasant five-minute stroll through the city streets, the café came into view. The quaint exterior, just as Caleb had described, was even more charming in the soft, morning light. As they approached, the inviting aroma of coffee and baked goods filled the air, making their stomachs rumble in anticipation.

The vibrant flowers that adorned the outdoor seating area added a splash of color against the café's rustic façade, making the place look even more inviting. As they neared, the sounds of soft music and distant chatter grew louder, a testament to the café's popularity among the locals.

Caleb held the door open for Meghan, a soft smile playing on his lips as he gestured for her to go inside. Their breakfast date was about to begin, and they both looked forward to the shared moments and stories that awaited them.

As they stepped into the café, the warmth from the bustling kitchen and the hum of quiet conversations enveloped them. They spotted a secluded corner table, the perfect spot for their breakfast date. Caleb led the way, pulling out the chair for Meghan in a gentlemanly gesture. She thanked him with a smile, settling comfortably into her seat.

A waitress approached their table, notepad and pen in hand, ready to take their order. Her professional smile never wavered as she patiently waited for them to make their selection.

"Meghan," Caleb turned towards her, "may I order for you?" His tone was respectful, ensuring she was comfortable with him making the decisions. Meghan's response was a warm smile, "Yes, please." She trusted his judgement, curious to see what he would choose for their breakfast. Caleb returned her smile, then turned towards the waitress, ready to place their order. Their breakfast date was in full swing, each moment deepening the connection between them.

Caleb turned to the waitress, his demeanor confident as he began to speak in fluent Italian, "Avremo due frittate a colazione, due espressi con crema italiana." His words flowed with ease, the language rolling naturally off his tongue.

The waitress nodded, jotting down the order. The order translated to two breakfast frittatas and two Italian espressos with cream. A delightful choice for their breakfast date. Meghan looked impressed; her eyes lit up in appreciation for Caleb's linguistic skills. With their order placed, the pair settled in, looking forward to enjoying their Italian breakfast and the rest of their morning together.

After a short wait, the waitress returned, skillfully balancing a tray laden with their breakfast. She set down the steaming espressos and generously filled frittatas in front of them, the delicious aroma wafting up and making their mouths water. The breakfast looked just as good as it smelled. The frittatas were golden and fluffy, filled with an assortment of fresh vegetables, while the espressos were topped with a perfect layer of creamy froth.

As they began to eat, the conversation naturally flowed to their plans for the day. They discussed various options, their likes and interests shaping the day's itinerary. From wandering through local museums, to exploring charming city parks, to simply walking along the bustling city streets, they found joy in planning their day together.

The café's ambiance provided the perfect backdrop for their conversation, a blend of comfort and intimacy that reflected their growing connection. As they sipped their espressos and savored their breakfast, Meghan and Caleb looked forward to the day ahead, excited about the memories they were about to create.

After a leisurely breakfast, Caleb and Meghan left the café, their bodies warmed by the delicious food and their spirits lifted by the engaging conversation. Their next stop was the museum, a place where they could continue to share experiences and learn more about each other's tastes and perspectives.

As they walked side by side, their pace matched perfectly, they admired the city around them. The streets were alive with activity, but in their shared company, it felt as if they were in their own intimate bubble.

The museum was not far from the café, and the short walk was filled with more conversation and laughter. Upon reaching the museum, they paused to admire the grand architecture, a promise of the cultural treasures that lay within. With a sense of shared anticipation, they stepped into the museum, ready to delve into the history and art that awaited them. The day was turning out to be as delightful as their breakfast, and they looked forward to the shared exploration and conversations the museum visit would inspire.

As the hour edged towards 12 o'clock, their morning exploration of the museum was punctuated by the gentle rumble of their stomachs. Caleb turned to Meghan, his eyes asking the question before his words did, "Are you ready to have lunch?" Meghan's response was a radiant smile, "Yes, lunch sounds great!", her words were accompanied by a feeling of contentment. Their morning had been filled with shared laughter, engaging conversations, and mutual interests.

As they made their way to a local trattoria, Meghan couldn't help but reflect on the man beside her. Caleb was indeed charming and undoubtedly gorgeous, but what she found most appealing was the way he made her feel. He made her feel valued, respected, and cared for. His every action, from the way he held the door open for her to the way he attentively listened to her stories, reflected his genuine interest in her.

There in the romantic city of Venice, Meghan found herself deeply drawn to Caleb, not just for his good looks, but for his kind heart and captivating personality. The day was not yet over, and she looked forward to spending more time with him, cherishing every moment of their time together.

Caleb looked at Meghan as they leisurely walked towards the local trattoria, her question lingering in the air between them, "Caleb, what brings you to Venice:"

He paused a moment, his eyes reflecting the warm sunlight as he considered her question. "Well, Meghan," he began, his voice soft yet filled with a sense of adventure, "I've always been drawn to places rich in history and culture. Venice, with its beautiful canals, stunning architecture, and vibrant art scene, has always been on my list."

He glanced at Meghan, a warm smile playing on his lips, "But I must say, the city has become even more captivating with you by my side." His admission was sincere, his words echoing the connection they both felt growing stronger with each shared moment. Their journey through Venice was just beginning, and they both eagerly anticipated the memories they were yet to create.

As they strolled through the romantic streets of Venice, a turmoil brewed within Caleb. He knew that Meghan would inevitably ask about his origins. His truth was not one easily swallowed; he hailed from another galaxy, a reality that could easily frighten or alienate her. Yet, he respected Meghan too much to weave a web of lies.

His gaze flitted to her, observing her radiant smile and the way her eyes sparkled with interest. He pondered on how she would react to his outlandish truth. Would she recoil in fear? Would she regard him differently? He resolved to let the day unfold as it was meant to. When the time was ripe, he would share his truth. All he could do was hope that she would accept him, in spite of his extraterrestrial origins. For the time being, he chose to concentrate on the present, on the captivating woman beside him, and on the enchanting allure of Venice.

As the charming trattoria came into view, Caleb instinctively wrapped his arm around Meghan's waist, drawing her closer to him. The gesture was natural, a subtle affirmation of the bond that was deepening between them. Meghan responded in kind, her arm snaking around his waist as she leaned into him. Her smile was bright, her eyes twinkling with warmth and happiness. She found comfort in his presence, his arm around her waist a reassuring anchor in this foreign city.

Their bodies swayed in rhythm as they walked, their steps in sync. This shared moment, though simple, was intimate and special. As they neared their lunch destination, both Meghan and Caleb reveled in the closeness, eagerly anticipating the rest of their day together.

Upon reaching the quaint trattoria, Caleb, ever the gentleman, held the door open for Meghan. She smiled in appreciation, stepping inside the warm, welcoming establishment. Caleb followed closely behind, his presence a comforting constant. The trattoria was a cozy place, filled with the inviting scent of Italian cuisine and the cheerful hum of conversation.

As they took their seats, they both appreciated the rustic charm of the trattoria. The worn wooden tables, the checkered tablecloths, and the soft, ambient lighting all contributed to a sense of romance and coziness.

With the promise of a delicious meal and more shared experiences ahead, Meghan and Caleb settled in, ready to continue their delightful day in the enchanting city of Venice. Soon after they had settled into their seats, a friendly waitress approached their table. In her hands, she held two menus, their pages filled with the mouthwatering promise of traditional Italian cuisine. With a warm smile, she handed them each a menu, her professional demeanor exuding a warm, hospitable charm. As she left them to peruse the options, Meghan and Caleb dove into the task at hand.

Together, they navigated through the menu, discussing the various dishes, sharing their preferences, and occasionally asking each other for suggestions. It was a simple act, but one that further highlighted their growing connection and mutual respect. As they awaited the waitress's return to take their order, they reveled in the shared anticipation of the delectable meal to come.

When the waitress returned, she greeted them with a warm smile, her question resonating in the cozy trattoria, "Cosa posso regalarti oggi?" – What can I bring you today?

Caleb responded with ease; his command of the Italian language evident. "Inizieremo con un antipasto, la caprese. E per il nostro pasto, io avro i tagliolini al salmone e lei avra i ravioli panna e funghi. Due te dolci, per favore." Their order, filled with traditional Italian dishes, translated to starting with a Caprese appetizer, followed by Tagliolini with salmon for him and ravioli with cream and mushrooms for her, ending with two sweet teas.

The waitress jotted down their order, her nod of approval signaling her appreciation for their excellent meal choices. As she left to relay their order to the kitchen, Meghan and Caleb sat back, their anticipation for the meal heightened by the delicious aromas wafting from the kitchen. Their day in Venice was only getting better.

As they waited for their meal, Meghan turned to Caleb, her curiosity piqued. "Do you travel a lot?" she asked, her eyes meeting his. Caleb's smile was gentle, tinged with a hint of mystery. He knew that this question was inching closer to the truth he had been contemplating how to reveal. He decided to answer honestly, but carefully.

"Yes, I do travel quite a bit," he began, his voice steady. "I've always been fascinated by different cultures, histories, and cuisines. Traveling gives me a chance to learn, to experience, and to grow. He paused; his gaze still locked with hers. "But no matter where I go, I find that what truly makes a place special are the people I meet and the connections I make. Like right now, being here in Venice with you has made this trip more memorable than any I've had before."

His words hung in the air, a testament to the bond they were forming. While he hadn't revealed his full truth yet, he hoped that he had laid a strong enough foundation of trust and respect to weather whatever reaction Meghan might have when he eventually did.

"I haven't been to very many places," Meghan admitted, her gaze drifting out of the trattoria's window, as if she could see her dream destination in the distance. "But one place I have always wanted to visit is Egypt." She turned back to Caleb, her curiosity sparking again. "Do you have a favorite place that you have visited?"

Caleb didn't hesitate. "Absolutely, Venice, Italy." His words were met with Meghan's surprised expression, and he couldn't help the smile that played on his lips. "Because I met you here." His words were simple but filled with sincerity. Meghan felt her cheeks warm, a blush creeping in at his admission. His honesty, his charm, and his caring nature were making this trip to Venice more memorable than she could have ever imagined. As they continued to wait for their meal, the connection between them deepened, their shared experiences in the city of canals becoming an unforgettable chapter in their lives.

The moment their lunch arrived, carried by the friendly waitress, the enticing scent of Italian cuisine filled the air around them. Both Meghan and Caleb watched as the plates were carefully placed before them, the beautifully presented dishes offering a feast for the eyes as well as the palate.

Meghan was the first to comment, her eyes wide with delight. "Oh, this looks and smells delicious," she exclaimed, her excitement palpable.
Her gaze flitted from her dish of ravioli panna e funghi to Caleb's tagliolini al salmone, both dishes exuding and irresistible allure. Caleb nodded in agreement, his own anticipation for the meal heightened by Meghan's enthusiastic reaction.
As they prepared to dig into their lunch, they shared a look of mutual appreciation, not just for the food, but for the shared experience, the memories being made, and the connection growing stronger between them.

As they savored their delicious Italian meal, conversation flowed naturally between Caleb and Meghan. Their topic of choice: Meghan's fascination with Egypt. Her enthusiasm was infectious as she discussed her interest in ancient civilization. "I've always been intrigued by Egypt's rich history," she began, her eyes sparkling with passion. "The pyramids, the pharaohs, the hieroglyphs. It's a culture that's so ancient, yet so advanced for its time."

Caleb listened attentively, his gaze never leaving Meghan's animated face as she delved deeper into her interest. She talked about her fascination with the mystery of the pyramids, her desire to see the Sphinx up close, and her dream of drifting down the Nile. Her passion was evident, and Caleb found himself captivated, not just by her words, but by the way her face lit up as she spoke about her dream destination.

As they continued to eat, the conversation drifted from Egypt to other topics, their connection deepening with every shared laugh, every mutual interest discovered, and every new memory created.

Once their satisfying meal had come to an end, Caleb turned to Meghan with a proposition. "Would you like to go tour the Sistine Chapel?" he asked, his eyes gleaming with anticipation. He knew that visiting the iconic chapel would be an unforgettable experience, a chance for them to appreciate the breathtaking art and history together. It was another adventure waiting to happen, another memory to be made in their shared journey through the enchanting city of Venice.

Meghan's response, whether filled with excitement or surprise, would be the next step in their unfolding adventure. Caleb waited for her answer, his heart filled with hope and anticipation. This day, he knew, was becoming more special with every passing moment. Meghan's face lit up at the suggestion, her excitement mirroring Caleb's. "I would love to," she exclaimed, her eyes sparkling. "It's one place I haven't seen since I have been here!"

Her enthusiasm was infectious, and Caleb couldn't help but share in her joy. He was delighted that he could contribute to making her experience in Italy even more memorable. With that, they left the cozy trattoria, their hearts filled with anticipation for their next adventure. As they made their way towards the Sistine Chapel, they both knew that this day, already filled with mesmerizing sights and shared experiences, was only going to get better. Their journey through Venice was turning out to be a series of unforgettable moments, and they were eager to see what the rest of the day had in store for them.

As they approached the Sistine Chapel, the grandeur of the iconic structure came into view. The sun's rays illuminated the intricate architectural details, casting a heavenly glow on the historic building. Meghan was clearly in awe, her eyes wide and sparkling with admiration. "It's breathtaking," she whispered, as if speaking too loudly might shatter the enchanting scene before them. Her gaze roamed over the façade of the chapel, taking in the splendor and the centuries-old craftsmanship.

Caleb watched Meghan's reaction, his heart swelling with joy. He knew the inside of the chapel, with its awe-inspiring frescoes, would be even more impressive. As they moved closer to the entrance, they shared a look of mutual anticipation, excited about the art and history that awaited them inside.

As Caleb and Meghan stepped inside the Sistine Chapel, the grandeur of the interior enveloped them. High above them, the vast ceiling painted by Michelangelo loomed, a masterpiece of art and history that had stood the test of centuries. Meghan's reaction was immediate. She gasped silently, her breath hitching in her throat as she took in the remarkable sight. Her eyes scanned the vast expanse of the frescoed ceiling, tracing the familiar scenes of Genesis that were depicted with such intricate detail.

Caleb watched Meghan, her awe-struck expression mirroring the reverence he had felt the first time he had seen the chapel. It was a moment of shared appreciation, a memory etched in time that they would both carry with them long after their journey in Venice came to an end.

As the day wore on and the sun began to dip below the horizon, painting the sky in hues of pink and orange, Caleb turned to Meghan. "What would you like to do next?" he asked, his gaze soft in the fading light. Meghan's response was accompanied by a warm smile. "Maybe," she began, her voice tinged with a hint of shyness, "you could come back to my hotel suite, and we could watch a movie together?"

Caleb's heart fluttered at her suggestion. It was an intimate invitation, a chance to spend more time together away from the bustling streets of Venice. His smile matched hers as he nodded in agreement. "I'd like that," he said, his voice filled with genuine warmth.

As they made their way back to Meghan's hotel, the setting sun casting long shadows around them, they both knew that this day had been extraordinary. As they looked forward to their quiet evening together, they also knew that their shared journey in Venice was far from over.

As they ambled through the winding streets of Venice, their hands fitting comfortably together, Caleb was lost in a whirlpool of thoughts. The truth he had been wrestling with revealing to Meghan all day continued to gnaw at him. He wasn't just an ordinary traveler exploring Italy; he hailed from a distant galaxy, far beyond the confines of Earth. His encounter with Meghan had been unanticipated, a chance meeting that had blossomed into something beautifully profound and unexpectedly significant.

Silence enveloped them as they walked, the dwindling sunlight casting a warm, ethereal glow on their figures. Caleb knew he could no longer allow their budding relationship to develop on a foundation of half-truths and veiled realities.

Glancing at Meghan, her face bathed in the soft, golden light, her hand nestled comfortably in his, Caleb felt a pang of apprehension. His revelation could drastically change their dynamics, but he also understood the importance of honesty in this delicate situation. As they continued their leisurely stroll, Caleb mentally prepared himself for the revealing conversation that awaited them, hoping that their newfound connection could withstand the shock of his unearthly origin.

When they finally reached the hotel lobby, Caleb paused, looking at Meghan with a thoughtful expression. "Are you sure about this?", he asked, his voice gentle. "I don't want to impose on you." Meghan's response was immediate and warm. Her smile was reassuring as she squeezed his hand, a gesture filled with affection and sincerity. "Yes, I want to spend more time with you," she said, her words echoing in the quiet lobby.

Her reassurance was a balm to Caleb's worries, and he felt a wave of relief wash over him. His heart swelled with happiness as he followed Meghan to the elevator, their hands still entwined. The evening was far from over, and he was eager to spend more time with her, even if the looming conversation was still casting a shadow over his thoughts.

As they ascended in the plush elevator, Meghan began to describe her hotel suite to Caleb. Her words painted a picture of opulence and comfort, her excitement palpable in her voice. "It's a beautiful suite," she started, her eyes sparkling with enthusiasm. "It has everything you could possibly need. A spacious living room with a panoramic view of the city, a kitchenette stocked with gourmet snacks, a plush king-size bed, and a bathroom that is practically a spa."

As she spoke, Caleb could picture the suite in his mind, from the abundant comforts to the stunning views. It sounded like a haven, a place where one could easily lose track of time. He smiled at Meghan, his eyes reflecting his appreciation. "Sounds like a dream," he remarked, his curiosity piqued. As the elevator doors opened to reveal the opulent corridor leading to Meghan's suite, Caleb couldn't help but feel a sense of anticipation. The evening was turning out to be full of surprises, and he was eager to see what else was in store.

As Meghan unlocked the door and pushed it open, Caleb was greeted with a sight that left him in awe. The suite was a masterpiece of luxury and elegance, surpassing even the vivid picture Meghan had painted with her words. The living room was flooded with the soft glow of the setting sun, casting long shadows across the plush furnishings. The view from the panoramic window was breathtaking, offering a stunning vista of the enchanting city. The kitchenette was stocked with an array of gourmet snacks and the bedroom, visible from where he stood, boasted a king-size bed that promised utmost comfort. "Wow," Caleb breathed, his eyes wide with admiration. "You weren't kidding. This place is incredible." He stepped inside, still marveling at the luxurious surroundings. As Meghan closed the door behind them, Caleb felt a sense of contentment wash over him. Despite the secrets he was yet to reveal, he was looking forward to the evening ahead, enjoying Meghan's company in such a remarkable setting.

"So, what movie should we watch?", Caleb asked, glancing at Meghan, his tone light and playful. Meghan's response was immediate and cheeky, her eyes sparkling with mischief. "How about 'Dirty Dancing'?", she suggested, her smile infectious. Caleb couldn't help but laugh at her choice, his heart warming at her playful demeanor. "Dirty Dancing, huh?", he echoed, raising an eyebrow in amusement. "I must say, I didn't see that coming. But it's a classic, so why not?"

With their movie decided, they settled comfortably into the plush living room, the glow from the city lights filtering in through the panoramic window, setting a cozy ambiance. As the opening credits of 'Dirty Dancing' began to play, they both knew they were in for a memorable evening.

As the movie progressed, capturing their attention with its iconic scenes, Meghan turned to Caleb, a dreamy look in her eyes. "I've always wanted to learn some of those dances," she confessed, her gaze lingering on the screen where the characters swayed to the rhythm of the music. Caleb looked at her, a smile playing on his lips. The thought of Meghan attempting those dances was endearing, and he couldn't help but imagine them both trying to replicate the steps in the spacious living room of her suite.

"Really?", he asked, his tone teasing. "Well, who knows, maybe tonight is the night you learn the mambo or the cha-cha." The playful challenge hung in the air between them, making the evening even more thrilling. As Caleb's words hung in the air, Meghan turned and met his gaze. Her eyes sparkled with a mixture of excitement and anticipation. Slowly, she reached out, her fingers weaving through his in a gentle, intimate gesture. Caleb's heart pounded in his chest as he leaned in, his breath hitching as their faces drew closer. The world seemed to slow down, the movie fading into the background as he focused solely on Meghan.

Their lips finally met in a passionate kiss, a culmination of the connection they had been building since their encounter in the Sistine Chapel. It was a moment of pure intimacy, their surroundings forgotten as they lost themselves in each other.

Caleb reluctantly pulled away from Meghan, his heart pounding in his chest. He looked into her eyes, his own filled with a mixture of regret and determination. "I can't let you do this right now," he said, his voice barely more than a whisper. "I need to tell you something, and I hope you can have an open mind about it."

Caleb took a deep breath, preparing himself for the revelation that could change everything. His hands tightened around hers, drawing comfort from the warmth of her touch. "I am not from this world, Meghan," he confessed, his voice steady despite the turmoil within him. "I hail from a distant galaxy, worlds away from Earth."

He watched her face carefully, his heart pounding with anxiety. Revealing his origin was risky, but he believed in their connection. He hoped that she would understand that the bond they had formed would withstand this incredible revelation. As he continued to hold her gaze, he waited for Meghan's reaction, hoping against hope that she would accept the truth.

Meghan's initial reaction was one of disbelief, her laughter light as she responded, "You're joking, right?" But as she looked into his eyes, her smile faded. The fear and vulnerability she saw there were unmistakable. It made her heart clench, the realization dawning on her that he was being honest. She was silent for a moment, her mind racing to process what Caleb had just revealed. It was an incredible, almost unbelievable claim, yet the sincerity in his eyes, the earnestness in his voice, convinced her that he was speaking the truth.

Wrapping her fingers tighter around his, she gave him a small, reassuring smile. The revelation was a lot to take in, but she wasn't going to let it change the connection they had formed. It was a strange and unexpected twist, but she trusted and felt safe with him. It only made their story all the more unique and she was eager to understand more, to delve deeper into the enigma that was Caleb.

"Okay," Meghan said, her voice a little shaky as she tried to process the information. "Umm…".

Caleb, sensing her uncertainty, quickly jumped in to reassure her. "I would never do anything to hurt you, Meghan," he said earnestly. "I wanted to be honest with you."

Meghan looked at him, her mind still grappling with the revelation. Then, slowly, her lips curved into a small smile. "So, you're an alien from outer space?", she asked, her voice filled with a mixture of disbelief and curiosity. "And you really do have a spaceship?"

Caleb nodded, relieved to see her taking the news relatively well. Meghan's smile widened as she added, "Okay…I'm intrigued." Her reaction was a load off Caleb's shoulders. The evening had taken an unexpected turn, but Meghan's open-mindedness and curiosity gave him hope. Their journey was far from over, and he was looking forward to exploring this new aspect of their relationship.

"Can I see it?", Meghan asked, her voice barely above a whisper. A blush spread across her cheeks at Caleb's raised eyebrow. "Your spaceship, I mean." Caleb couldn't help but chuckle at her eagerness, his heart swelling with affection. He appreciated her curiosity and her willingness to indulge in his otherworldly reality.

"Of course, Meghan," he replied, his eyes twinkling under the soft glow of the room's lights. "But it is not here in Venice. It's cloaked and in a safe location outside of the city. We can go see it tomorrow if you'd like." Meghan's face lit up at his words, her excitement palpable. This unexpected turn of events had certainly added a thrilling twist to their blossoming relationship, and they were both eager to explore this new chapter together.

Caleb looked at Meghan, his expression softening. "I'm just happy that you didn't run away screaming," he admitted. "I didn't want to scare you." His words were heartfelt, his relief palpable. Meghan had not only accepted his revelation but was also curious to know more. It was more than he could've hoped for.

Meghan reached out, gently squeezing his hand in reassurance. "It's a lot to take in, Caleb," she said, her voice gentle. "But I'm not scared, I trust you. I want to understand more." Her acceptance was a balm to Caleb's fears, and he felt a wave of gratitude wash over him. He was eager to share more about his origins, to let Meghan into his world, and he couldn't wait to see where this journey would lead them.

Meghan's smile was soft as she looked at Caleb, her fingers still entwined with his. "The last couple of days, I have been so happy spending time with you," she confessed, her gaze warm as she met his. "You truly are a gentleman; unlike any man I have ever known." Her words were sincere, her admiration for him clear in her eyes. Despite the shocking revelation, she was glad to have met Caleb, glad to have embarked on this unusual journey with him.

Caleb felt a surge of warmth in her words, his heart fluttering in his chest. "Meghan," he said, his voice filled with emotion. "I feel the same way about you. You're unlike anyone I've ever met. I'm glad we crossed paths."

As they shared this moment of mutual admiration, the evening seemed to take on a new significance. Despite the unexpected events, they were both excited about what the future held for them.

Meghan's mischievous smile was infectious, causing Caleb to laugh as she quipped, "Now I know why you are such a great kisser." Caleb's laughter was hearty, his eyes twinkling with amusement. "Oh, is that so?", he teased, his gaze softening as he looked at her. "And here I was thinking it was because of the romantic setting and the good company."

Their playful banter was a welcome distraction from the night's startling revelation, easing the tension and reinforcing the connection they had established. Despite the unexpected turn of events, their bond remained unshaken, their mutual attraction stronger than ever.

Meghan's question broke the comfortable silence that had settled between them. "Would you care for a drink?", she asked, gesturing towards the mini bar in the corner of the suite. "This suite comes with a fully stocked mini bar." Caleb turned to look at the mini bar, a small smile playing on his lips. "That sounds like a wonderful idea, Meghan," he replied, nodding in appreciation. "What do you recommend?"

Their conversation flowed naturally; the earlier tension forgotten as they delved into more mundane topics. The night was far from over, and they were determined to make the most of it, enjoying each other's company and the unique connection they shared.

Meghan glanced at the mini bar, assessing the various options before answering with a smile, "I like pina coladas myself." Meghan rose from her seat and moved over to the mini bar, fixing two pina coladas with practiced ease. She hands one to Caleb before settling back into her seat. Taking a sip of her own drink, she looked at Caleb with a playful smile. "Well, what do you think?", she asked.

Caleb took a sip of the pina colada Meghan had handed him. His eyes widened slightly in surprise before a smile formed on his lips, "I'm impressed," he admitted, holding up the glass in appreciation. "This is really good."

After finishing their drinks, Caleb glanced at the clock, noting the late hour. "It's getting late," he began, setting his empty glass down. "I better go and let you get some sleep." As he made a move to stand, Meghan reached out and took his hand in hers, her eyes meeting his. "Stay with me tonight," she requested softly, her gaze sincere and hopeful.

Caught off guard by her request, Caleb looked at Meghan, his eyes searching hers. "Are you sure?" he asked, his voice laced with surprise and a hint of concern. In response, Meghan leaned in and kissed him, her actions speaking louder than any words could. The surprise in Caleb's eyes softened into understanding and he returned her kiss, his initial hesitation fading away.

Gently squeezing Caleb's hand, Meg looked into his eyes with genuine interest. "Caleb," she began, her voice soft in the quiet room, "I find myself increasingly intrigued by you. I would love to delve deeper into your past, understand your roots. Tell me more about where you come from?",

Caleb met Meghan's gaze, his eyes reflecting a depth of sincerity. "Meghan," he began, his voice steady and warm, "I would be more than willing to open up about my past, about the places I've been and the experiences I have had." He gave her hand a gentle squeeze and continued, "But it's not just about me. I find myself equally, if not more, interested in understanding your story. I want to know about your dreams, your aspirations, and the moments that have defined you. I would love to learn about the path you've walked to become the person you are, about the challenges you've overcome and the victories you've celebrated. Because, Meghan, understanding you is as important to me as sharing my own story."

Holding Caleb's gaze, Meghan gave his hand a reassuring squeeze. The corners of her mouth curled up into a soft smile, her eyes sparkling with anticipation and a hint of vulnerability. The room around them seemed to melt away, leaving only the two of them in their shared moment of intimacy. "So," she began, her voice steady yet tinged with a hopeful note, "does that mean you've decided to stay here with me tonight?" Her question hung in the air between them, their connection deepening in the silence that followed, as they both waited for his response. Looking deeply into Meghan's eyes, Caleb nodded, his decision firm. "Yes," he finally said, his voice soft but resolute. "If that's what you want, I'll stay."

With that, they settled into the comfortable couch, their hands still intertwined. The conversation flowed easily between them, marked by laughter, contemplative silence, and shared stories. They spoke about where they were from, their families or the lack of, and their childhood memories, and the experiences that had shaped them into who they were today.

They lost track of time, talking and sharing until the first rays of dawn peeked in through the window. The night had passed, but they were content, knowing that they had shared something meaningful and had grown closer in the process.

Caught up in their conversation, Caleb hadn't noticed the subtle shift in the room's lighting. He glanced towards the window and was surprised by the soft morning glow filtering in. "Is it really morning already?", he asked, his voice tinged with disbelief and a hint of amusement. In response, Meghan rose from the couch, her hand still holding his. She gently tugged him up and led him towards the suite's bedroom, the early morning light casting a warm glow around them. Once in the room, she wrapped her arms around Caleb's neck, pulling him closer. The world outside seemed to fade away as she tilted her head up to meet his and kissed him, marking the beginning of a new day.

Caleb took a deep breath, fully aware of the intimate direction their connection was taking. He gently pulled back, just enough to look into Meghan's eyes – those beautiful eyes that held a universe he was only beginning to explore. As if reading his thoughts, Meghan offered him a reassuring smile. "Caleb," she whispered, her voice barely heard over the beating of his heart, "I'm okay with you being here with me, I want you here." Her words echoed in the stillness of the room, a silent affirmation of their deepening bond. She sealed her words with a soft kiss, creating an intimate promise between them.

Caleb responded by wrapping his arms around her waist, pulling her closer into his embrace. His heart pounded in his chest, the rhythm echoing the intensity of their connection. With practiced ease he slipped off Meghan's shirt, his lips trailing kisses down her neck as his fingers worked on undoing her bra.
As Meghan's hands slid under his shirt, he instinctively tensed, a shiver running down his spine at her touch. In one fluid motion, he lifted his arms and pulled his shirt off over his head, the fabric discarded somewhere in the dimly lit room. Their eyes met again, their connection unspoken but deeply felt, as they continued to explore this new intimacy between them.

  As Caleb pulled Meghan close again, the sensation of her bare skin against his chest sent a wave of exhilaration coursing through them both. The world outside ceased to exist, their universe shrinking to the space between their intertwined bodies. In a dance as old as time, they helped each other out of the rest of their clothes, their movements fluid and unhurried. Each article discarded on the floor was a testament to the trust and intimacy growing between them.

  With a strength that belied his gentle touch, Caleb picked Meghan up in his arms and gently laid her down on the king-sized bed. The soft sheets beneath them contrasted with the intensity of their connection as they continued to explore each other's bodies, their actions speaking volumes in the silence of the room. Each touch, each caress, was a promise of deepening intimacy, a testament to their shared desire.

  As the intensity between them continued to build, Caleb found himself lost in the depths of his desire for Meghan. Their bodies moved together in a dance of passion; their senses heightened by the intoxicating connection between them. In the privacy of their shared space, Caleb claimed Meghan as his in that moment, a silent pledge between them that echoed in the quiet of the room. Their connection deepened, marking the beginning of their shared journey into the realm of intimacy and desire.

  Time seemed to stand still, their world narrowing down to the shared rhythm of their hearts, as they climaxed together. The world outside ceased to exist, their universe shrinking to the space between their intertwined bodies. As they lay there spent, a sheen of perspiration on their skin, they tried to catch their breath, their chests rising and falling in tandem. The room was filled with a profound silence, punctuated only by their ragged breaths and the soft rustle of the sheets beneath them.

  After a few minutes, Caleb propped himself up on his elbow, his gaze softening as he looked at Meghan. He leaned in, pressing a gentle kiss to her lips, the tenderness of the gesture a stark contrast to the intensity of their previous actions. "Are you okay, Meghan?", he asked, his voice barely above a whisper, his concern for her well-being evident in his eyes.

  Meghan's smile radiated warmth as she snuggled closer to Caleb, her heart feeling full and content. "I'm more than okay," she murmured, her voice a soft melody in the quiet room. Caleb's gaze softened as he looked at her, a deep sense of connection shining in his eyes. "You belong to me, and I to you now," he affirmed, his words carrying a weight of commitment and love.

  In that moment, as they lay entwined in each other's arms, their bond deepened, their hearts intertwined in a promise of shared belonging and mutual love. The silence of the room enveloping them in a cocoon of intimacy, Caleb's thoughts drifted to a place of reflection. His fingers traced soft patterns on Meghan's skin, his touch gentle and reverent.

  In the quiet of the moment, a realization dawned on him. A deep sense of gratitude washed over him as he looked at Meghan, her presence a beacon of light in his life. How had he ever survived before he found her, he wondered, his heart overflowing with love and appreciation for the woman in his arms.

As the tranquility of the moment wrapped around them like a warm embrace, Caleb and Meghan found solace in each other's arms. The gentle rise and fall of their breaths harmonized, creating a soothing lullaby that carried them into realm of dreams.

Later that day, Caleb awakens to the gentle light filtering through the room, he shifted his gaze to Meghan, who was still asleep beside him. Watching her peaceful form, he couldn't help but feel a surge of gratitude for having found someone as special as her. The way she lay there, serene and beautiful, filled his heart with a sense of awe and wonder.

As if sensing his presence, Meghan stirred and slowly opened her eyes, a soft smile gracing her lips, as she looked at Caleb. Their eyes met, and in that moment, no words were needed to convey the depth of their connection. It was a silent acknowledgement of the love and bond they shared, a moment that spoke volumes in its simplicity and beauty. Caleb felt a sense of peace wash over him, knowing that he was truly blessed to have Meghan by his side.

As they both got up and dressed, Caleb and Meghan shared a moment of realization that they hadn't eaten anything yet that day. With a playful smile, Meghan turned to Caleb and asked, "So, can you conjure up some lunch for us?" Caleb chuckled at her request, a twinkle in his eyes as he considered the idea. "I think I can manage that," he replied, his tone teasing and light-hearted. With a wave of his hand and a mischievous grin, he conjured up a delicious spread of their favorite dishes, laid out before them as if by magic.

As they sat down to enjoy their impromptu meal, the laughter and joy that filled the room mirrored the warmth of their connection. In that moment, as they shared a simple meal together, Caleb and Meghan knew that they were not just nourishing their bodies but also feeding their souls with the love and companionship they shared.

After they finished their lunch, they stood out on the private balcony of Meghan's hotel suite, the soft breeze playing with their hair and the sun casting a warm glow around them, Caleb surreptitiously conjured a small lavender box in his hand, its contents a glittering diamond ring that sparkled like a star in the night sky. With a mix of nerves and excitement, Caleb turned to face Meghan, the love in his eyes shining brightly as he knelt down on one knee before her. In a voice filled with emotion, he asked the question that had been burning in his heart, "Meghan, will you marry me?"

As he opened the box to reveal the dazzling ring, the light catching the facets of the diamond, Meghan's eyes widened in surprise and joy. Her hand flew to her mouth, tears of happiness glistening in her eyes as she looked at Caleb in awe. Overwhelmed with emotion, Meghan nodded vigorously, her voice barely a whisper as she managed to say, "Yes, yes, a thousand times yes!" In that moment, Caleb and Meghan knew that their love was a bond that would last a lifetime.

With a wide smile that lit up his face, Caleb gently took Meghan's hand in his and slipped the sparkling engagement ring onto her finger. The diamond twinkled in the sunlight, casting a mesmerizing glow as it found its place on her delicate hand. As the ring settled into its rightful spot, a sense of completeness washed over them both. Caleb's eyes never leaving Meghan's, he marveled at the sight of the ring adorning her finger, a symbol of their love and commitment.

In that simple gesture of placing the ring on her finger, a new chapter began for Caleb and Meghan. Their hearts entwined in a promise of forever, they stood on the balcony, basking in the warmth of their shared love and the bright future that lay ahead of them.

Caleb gazed into Meghan's eyes, his voice filled with sincerity and love as he whispered, "Meghan, I love you with all my heart. I promise to cherish you for all eternity, to stand by your side through every joy and every challenge that life may bring."

Meghan's eyes shimmered with tears of happiness as she reached out to caress Caleb's cheek, feeling the depth of his words in her soul. In that moment, surrounded by the beauty of the setting sun and the promise of a future together, they shared a love that felt timeless and unbreakable.

With a tender smile and a gentle touch, Caleb sealed his vow with a kiss, their lips meeting in a silent promise of a love that would endure through all the seasons of their life. And in that sweet moment, as they stood on the balcony, wrapped in each other's embrace, Caleb and Meghan knew that their love was a gift to be cherished for all eternity.

Chapter 4

The next day brought a new adventure. Meghan, eager to start their life together, asked Caleb to take her to his spacecraft so she could check out of her hotel suite. With a gentle nod, Caleb assured her, "Of course, love. Just let me know when you're ready." Meghan, suffused with excitement, began to pack her belongings into the two suitcases she had brought with her. Each folded garment, each tucked away trinket, was a step closer to their shared future. After about an hour, Meghan turned to Caleb, her suitcases packed and ready. "I'm ready," she declared, her eyes sparkling with anticipation.

Caleb explained to Meghan that they would be teleporting to his spacecraft. "Just wrap your arms around my neck and don't let go," he instructed, his voice steady and reassuring. He was about to show her a part of his world, and he couldn't wait to see her reaction. As Meghan complied, a sense of exhilaration filled the room – they were about to embark on a new journey together.

As Caleb began to concentrate, a distinct hum filled the air, the energy around them shifting in preparation for the teleportation. Meghan, unsure of what to expect, buried her face in the crook of Caleb's neck, her arms tightening around him in instinctive response. Caleb could feel her small tremors of anticipation and offered reassuring words, "Just trust me, love." His voice was a soothing balm, a steady presence as the world around them started to change.

The room seemed to dissolve around them, their surroundings blurring into a whirl of colors before reforming into a completely different setting. The teleportation, while disconcerting for a first-timer, was over in a matter of seconds, leaving them standing in the heart of Caleb's spacecraft. Caleb's voice broke through Meghan's apprehension, a beacon of reassurance amidst the unfamiliarity. "It's okay, we're here," he murmured into her ear, his warm breath a comforting presence.

Meghan slowly lifted her head from the crook of Caleb's neck, her eyes fluttering open to take in their new surroundings. She found herself standing in the midst of rooms that were the epitome of luxury, with intricate designs gracing every corner and surfaces gleaming with opulence. She stood in awe, her eyes wide as she took in the beauty around her. The grandeur of the spacecraft was like nothing else she had ever seen, an ethereal blend of modernity and elegance. It was a testament to Caleb's taste and his desire to provide her with the best.

Her heart swelled with love and gratitude for Caleb. This was their home now, a place where they would build countless memories together. As she turned to Caleb, her eyes shone with unshed tears, a silent thank you for the wonderful life he was about to give her. Caleb, with a warm smile on his face, took Meghan's hand and began to guide her through the spacecraft, showing her each room and explaining its functions. The tour was a blend of the familiar and the extraordinary, with each room revealing new facets of Calebs life.

They moved from the living area to the kitchen, then to the study and the bedrooms, each room more magnificent than the last. Meghan was captivated by the advanced technology seamlessly integrated with luxurious comfort, her mind buzzing with the possibilities each room presented. However, as they neared one particular room, Caleb's demeanor changed slightly. This was the control room, the heart of his vessel, and a place where Meghan shouldn't tread without him. "This is the control room," he told her, his voice serious. "Please don't go in here without me."

His request was born out of concern for Meghan's safety. The control room was filled with complex machinery and systems that could be dangerous if mishandled. Meghan nodded in understanding, her hand squeezing his in reassurance. She respected his boundaries and trusted him to keep her safe. Their shared home was filled with love and understanding, a testament to their strong bond.

With a playful twinkle in his eyes, Caleb turned to Meghan, his hand still holding hers. "Now," he began, his voice light and teasing, "whenever you pick a venue for our wedding, we can be there in minutes." His words brought a new wave of excitement. The reality of their situation – the ability to teleport anywhere in the world in a matter of minutes – was a thrilling prospect. The world was truly their oyster, and they could choose to hold their wedding in the most exotic of locations if they wished.

Meghan's eyes lit up at the idea, her mind already spinning with possibilities. A beach wedding in the Maldives, a castle wedding in Scotland, or a vineyard wedding in Italy – the options were endless. With Caleb's spacecraft, their wedding planning had just taken an exciting turn. The idea of being able to teleport to any location added a layer of magic to their wedding preparations, making the event even more special.

Meghan looked up at Caleb, her eyes sparkling with excitement. "Maybe a castle wedding?", she suggested, her voice filled with a mixture of hope and curiosity. She wanted to know his opinion, to make sure he was as excited about the idea as she was. Caleb's eyes lit up at her suggestion, the thought of a castle wedding conjuring images of grandeur and fairy-tale romance. "A castle wedding sounds magical," he agreed, his tone enthusiastic. "We could look at castles in Scotland, or perhaps Ireland or France. Wherever you wish, love."

His support brought a bright smile to Meghan's face. The idea of a castle wedding, one straight out of a fairy-tale, was becoming more and more appealing. They could exchange their vows in a centuries-old castle, surrounded by history and grandeur. It was a dream come true, and she couldn't wait to start planning.

Meghan's smile took on a mischievous edge as she threw out another suggestion, "Ummm...even in Transylvania, Romania?" Caleb's laughter echoed through the room, a rich sound filled with surprise and delight. He hadn't expected such an unconventional suggestion, but the idea was intriguing. "Transylvania?", he repeated, his eyes twinkling with amusement. "Now that would be a wedding to remember!"

The idea of a wedding in the legendary land of Transylvania, with its ancient castles and rich folklore, was certainly unique. It promised a blend of romance and adventure that was perfectly in tune with their extraordinary love story. As they laughed together, the prospect of a Transylvanian wedding adding a dose of excitement to their plans, Caleb and Meghan felt their connection deepen. Their love was as unique and thrilling as the wedding they were planning, and they wouldn't have it any other way.

In the weeks that followed, joy and laughter became a constant soundtrack in Caleb and Meghan's lives as they embarked on the journey of planning their wedding. The air was thick with anticipation and love, their shared excitement coloring every moment they spent together.

Caleb, ever the doting fiancé, told Meghan she could have any type of wedding she desired, in any location she chose. His power allowed him to conjure anything, no matter how grand or intricate, and he was more than willing to use it to make Meghan's dreams come true. He wanted to give her the world, for in his eyes, she was his world.

Meghan had become more than just his partner – she was his goddess. He worshipped the ground she walked on, her happiness his highest priority. He cherished her and was committed to treating her as the divine being he believed her to be. From the choice of flowers to the wedding venue, every decision was made with Meghan's happiness in mind. The wedding was going to be a reflection of their love for each other – pure, unadulterated, and eternal. As they planned their special day, Caleb and Meghan reveled in the joy of their engagement, looking forward to a lifetime of shared love and companionship.

Meghan found herself in a whirlwind of decisions – the color scheme, the venue, the caterer. Each choice seemed more important than the last, and she found herself constantly turning to Caleb for his input. Yet, his responses were always the same, "I'm great with whatever you choose, my love."

At first, Meghan was a little taken aback by Caleb's nonchalance. However, she soon realized that his lack of opinion wasn't due to indifference but rather his absolute trust in her choices. He valued her happiness above all else and was willing to go along with whatever she chose, as long as it made her happy. It was a testament to their love for each other. Meghan found comfort in Caleb's unwavering support, and it only reinforced the bond they shared. As they continued to plan their wedding, each decision Meghan made was filled with love and anticipation for the joyous day to come.

Meghan, with a mischievous smile dancing on her lips, turned to Caleb and declared, "Well, then, I am leaving the choice of the catering service all up to you." Caleb's eyes widened in surprise, a playful protest forming on his lips. But before he could voice his thoughts, Meghan wrapped her arms around his neck and pressed her lips to his in a sweet, lingering kiss. Pulling back slightly, she met his gaze and whispered, "I trust your judgement, Caleb." Her words, sincere and full of faith, left him momentarily speechless.

Finally, Caleb relented with a hearty laugh, the sound echoing around them and adding to the joyous atmosphere. "Alright, alright," he conceded, a twinkle in his eyes. "I'll take care of the caterers." Teasingly, he added, "Just don't blame me if we end up with an all-pizza menu." Their shared laughter, a testament to their bond, filled the room as they continued on their journey towards their special day.

Meghan's thoughts returned to the idea of a Transylvanian wedding. With the idea firmly planted in her mind, Meghan decided to do some research before presenting it to Caleb. She was particularly interested in the possibility of having a medieval-themed wedding at Bran Castle, a historical landmark often associated with the legend of Dracula.

Armed with her laptop, Meghan lost herself in the world of medieval wedding planning. She read articles on medieval traditions, browsed photos of Bran Castle, and even looked up medieval wedding attire. She imagined their wedding in the grand, ancient castle, the atmosphere rich with history and romance. The guests would be dressed in medieval feast, and they would exchange their vows under the ancient arches of Bran Castle. It was a unique concept, but one she found increasingly appealing.

Once she had gathered enough information, she couldn't wait to share her findings with Caleb. She wanted to see his reaction and get his opinion on the medieval wedding idea. She was excited about the possibility and hoped he would be too.

After spending a couple of hours immersing herself in research, Meghan was ready to present her idea to Caleb. She had gathered a wealth of information about medieval weddings and Bran Castle, and she was excited to share her findings with him.

With her laptop open to display pictures of the castle, Meghan beckoned Caleb over. "I've been doing some research," she began, her voice filled with anticipation. "What do you think about a medieval wedding at Bran Castle in Transylvania?" She guided him through the information she had found – pictures of the castle, articles about medieval wedding traditions, even examples of medieval wedding attire. She painted a vivid picture of their potential wedding, complete with medieval costumes, traditional music, and the grandeur of Bran Castle as their backdrop.

As Meghan shared her vision, her eyes were bright with excitement. She watched Caleb's face closely, eager to see his reaction to her idea. This was a wedding like no other, a blend of history, romance, and adventure, and she hoped he would be as thrilled about it as she was.

Caleb listened attentively as Meghan shared her findings, his eyes widening in surprise at the depth of her research. As she painted a picture of their potential wedding, he found himself drawn into the magic of her vision. The idea of a medieval wedding at Bran Castle was unique, intriguing, and incredibly romantic.

When Meghan finished her presentation, Caleb was silent for a moment, taking in all the information. Finally, he broke into a wide grin, his eyes sparkling with excitement. "Meghan, that sounds like an incredible amount of fun!" he exclaimed. "And I can't wait to see you in a medieval wedding dress. You're going to look stunning!"

His enthusiastic response brought a beaming smile to Meghan's face. His approval and excitement were all she needed to hear. Their wedding was shaping up to be a one-of-a-kind event, a beautiful blending of their adventurous spirits and enduring love. The prospect of exchanging vows in a medieval castle in Transylvania filled them both with exhilaration, and they couldn't wait to start the preparations.

With Caleb's approval and shared excitement, Meghan couldn't help the joy that bubbled up within her. She beamed at him, her eyes shining with happiness and anticipation for their future. In a swift move, she wrapped her arms around his neck, pulling herself closer him. Her heart was pounding in her chest, her feelings for Caleb stronger than ever. She looked up at him, her eyes reflecting her love and admiration for him.

Without another word, she leaned in and pressed her lips against his, sealing their shared excitement and love with a passionate kiss. It was a promise of the extraordinary journey they were about to embark on together, a journey that would start with a grand wedding in a medieval castle.

After their tender moment, Meghan turned back to her laptop, pulling up images of medieval wedding dresses. She found designs in various shades, but the ones that had caught her eye were in a striking combination of black and purple. As she showed these images to Caleb, she watched his face for his reaction. The dresses she'd chosen were a far cry from the traditional white wedding gown; they were bold and unconventional, much like their own love story.

Caleb's eyes widened as he took in the designs, his gaze drawn to one particular dress. It was a stunning creation in black and purple, with intricate ruffles adding a touch of drama. He could already envision Meghan in it, her beauty amplified by the unconventional dress. "Damn, Meg," he murmured, his voice filled with awe and anticipation. "I really like the black and purple one with the ruffles. I can't wait to see you in that one."

His reaction brought a bright smile to Meghan's face. "I like that one too," she says with a thrill of anticipation at the thought of wearing the gorgeous gown on their wedding day, knowing it would be a sight Caleb would remember forever. Their wedding was shaping up to be as unique and unforgettable as their love story, and they couldn't wait for the big day.

With the decision about her own wedding dress seemingly settled, Meghan turned her attention to Caleb. A mischievous twinkle in her eyes, she said, "Now for your wedding attire…" Caleb chuckled, intrigued by the gleam in her eyes. He knew Meghan had something special in mind, and he was excited to see what she had found.

Meghan pulled up images of medieval men's attire – tunics with intricate embroidery, breeches, and cloaks in various shades. From rich purples to deep blacks, the images displayed an array of options that would perfectly match her own dress. As Meghan presented the options to Caleb, she watched his reaction closely. Just as she had done with her own dress, she wanted to ensure that Caleb was as excited and comfortable with his wedding attire. After all, this was their day, and they both deserved to feel their best.

Meghan's fingers moved over her laptop, scrolling through the various options before stopping at one particular design. It was a black and red vampire suit, complete with a fur-topped cape – daring yet fitting choice for their Transylvanian wedding. She turned the laptop towards Caleb, her eyes searching his for his reaction. "What do you think about this one?", she asked, pointing at the image on the screen. The suit was unconventional and bold, much like their own love story.

Caleb leaned in, his eyes scanning the image. The black and red suit was certainly unique, and the fur-topped cape added a touch of grandeur that was perfect for a wedding at Bran Castle. He could already imagine himself in it, standing next to Meghan in her stunning black and purple dress.

As he visualized the scene the scene, a wide grin spread across his face. "I love it, Meg," he said, his voice filled with excitement. "It's perfect for our wedding. I can't wait to wear it!" His enthusiastic approval brought a smile to Meghan's face, her heart swelling with joy at their shared excitement for their upcoming wedding.

Meghan couldn't help the smile that spread across her face at Caleb's enthusiastic response. His willingness to embrace her unconventional ideas, his shared excitement for their unique wedding, only made her love for him grow stronger.

She reached over, taking Caleb's hand in hers, her gaze meeting his. The love in her eyes was undeniable as she said, "You really are something else, you know that?" With a soft sigh, she continued, her voice filled with emotion, "And I can't wait to be your wife." The words hung in the air between them, filled with the promise of a future filled with love and adventure. As they sat there, hand in hand, they both felt a surge of anticipation for their wedding day – a day that would mark the beginning of their lifelong journey together.

Caleb's smile mirrored Meghan's as he looked at her, his heart filled with an overwhelming sense of love and gratitude. He knew he was the luckiest man alive to have someone like Meghan in his life, someone who embraced his quirks, shared his adventurous spirit, and loved him unconditionally.

Unable to contain his feelings any longer, he gently squeezed Meghan's hand, his gaze never leaving hers. "Meg," he began, his voice filled with emotion. "I need you to know just how much you mean to me." He paused for a moment, searching for the right words to convey the depth of his love for her. "You are my everything," he continued, his voice barely above a whisper. "You bring joy to my life, inspire me to be a better man, and make every day an adventure. I love you more than I could ever express."

His heartfelt confession filled the room, a testament to their enduring love. As he declared his love for Meghan, Caleb knew he was ready for the next step in their journey. He looked forward to their wedding day, when they would commit to a lifetime of love and adventure together.

With their wedding partially planned and their love reaffirmed, Caleb felt a familiar pang of hunger. The afternoon had slipped by as they'd lost themselves in planning their unique wedding. He gave Meghan's hand a gentle squeeze, his eyes twinkling with a playful light as he suggested, "Now, how about I fix us lunch?"

Meghan, also realizing her own hunger, responded with a nod and a smile. Closing her laptop, she agreed, "Lunch sounds great, Caleb." As Caleb moved into the kitchen to prepare their meal, Meghan felt a sense of contentment wash over her. Their love was strong and their future was filled with excitement. As she watched Caleb, she couldn't help but look forward to the day when they would finally say "I do" in the heart of Transylvania.

As Caleb busied himself in the kitchen, Meghan felt a sudden urge to join him. She got up from her seat, her heart filled with happiness as she walked towards him. Slipping her arm around his waist, she leaned into him, her smile bright. "Need any help?" she asked, her voice soft. Cooking was always more enjoyable when they did it together, every shared task a testament to their partnership.

Caleb looked down at Meghan, a warm smile spreading across his face. Her offer to help was yet another reminder of their shared life and the love they had for each other. With her by his side, even the simplest tasks became moments to cherish. As they prepared their lunch together, their laughter and shared glances filled the kitchen, a symbol of their enduring love and the life they were building together.

Lunch was filled with light conversation and laughter, a comfortable routine they had fallen into. Once they'd finished eating, they settled into a comfortable silence, enjoying each other's company. Suddenly, Meghan broke the silence with a statement that caught Caleb off guard. "You know, I have always wanted to have a big ranch someday," she said, her voice filled with whimsy. Caleb blinked in surprise, the image of Meghan in a cowboy hat and boots taking him by surprise. He pictured her rounding up cattle and riding on horseback across wide open fields, a sight that was both endearing and amusing.

The thought was so unexpected, so out of the blue, that he couldn't help but burst into laughter. The image of them on a ranch, a far cry from their current city life, was amusing and oddly appealing at the same time. "Oh, really?" he managed to say between laughs. "A ranch, huh? That's a new one. But you know what? I think you'd make a pretty good rancher, Meghan."

His words brought a smile to her face, her eyes sparkling with amusement. Even though it was just a whimsical thought, the idea of them on a ranch added another layer to their shared dreams. Who knew? Maybe one day they would swap the hustle and bustle of city life for the tranquility of a ranch. Only time would tell.

As Caleb responded to her whimsical thought, Meghan found herself picturing him in a cowboy hat and boots, tight jeans, and no shirt. The image was so vivid, so different from the Caleb she knew, that she couldn't help but gasp quietly. Caleb, noticing her sudden change in demeanor, turned to her with a mischievous grin. "What are you thinking about, Meghan?" he asked, his eyes sparkling with curiosity.

Caught off guard by his question, Meghan could feel her cheeks heat up. The image of Caleb as a shirtless cowboy was still fresh in her mind, and she wasn't quite ready to share that with him. In an attempt to brush it off, she quickly said, "Oh, nothing…nothing at all." Her blush deepened, betraying her words.

Caleb chuckled, knowing full well she was hiding something. But he decided to let it go, instead playfully nudging her as they cleaned up after their meal. Their shared dreams, their laughter, their love – it all made their day-to-day life a constant adventure, and Caleb wouldn't have it any other way.

Meghan couldn't help the smile that tugged at her lips as she bit her bottom lip. Her thoughts were racing, the image of Caleb as a shirtless cowboy still vivid in her mind. She was glad that Caleb didn't press her further on her thoughts, giving her the space to keep her amusing fantasy to herself. "Thank goodness he can't read minds," she thought, her smile growing wider.

As they finished cleaning up after their meal, Meghan couldn't help but steal glances at Caleb. She found herself looking at him in a new light, her mind superimposing a cowboy hat onto his head. The thought brought a new wave of amusement, and she couldn't help but chuckle to herself. Yes, their future was filled with endless possibilities – whether they would end up in a castle in Transylvania or on a ranch, only time would tell. But one thing was for certain – as long as they were together, they would continue to make each other laugh, share their dreams, and love each other unconditionally. And for Meghan, that was all that mattered.

Caleb couldn't help but notice Meghan's barely audible chuckle, her eyes sparkling with amusement. His curiosity piqued, he walked up behind her, wrapping his arms around her waist. He leaned in, his warm breath ghosting over her ear as he grinned. "Okay, Meghan," he said, his voice laced with amusement and curiosity. "You have to tell me what you were thinking. Obviously, it's still fresh on your mind."

Meghan could feel her cheeks heating up again. She couldn't believe she was about to share her silly fantasy with Caleb. She took a deep breath, her heart pounding in her chest. "Promise you won't laugh?" she asked her voice barely a whisper. Caleb tightened his hold on her, his laughter rumbling through his chest. "I promise, babe," he said, his voice filled with anticipation. "Now, out with it. What's got you so flustered?"

Meghan took another deep breath, readying herself to share her amusing thought with Caleb. She just hoped he would find it as funny as she did. "Okay, okay," Meghan finally gave in, her cheeks turning a deeper shade of red. "I pictured you as a shirtless cowboy...in boots and a hat."

Caleb blinked in surprise for a moment before a wide grin spread across his face. He stepped back, his eyes twinkling with mischief. Before Meghan could react, he used his power to transform his attire, appearing in front of her just as she had envisioned him in her mind.

"Like this, Meghan?" he asked, his voice filled with amusement. He twirled around, showing off his cowboy boots and hat. The sight of him embracing her whimsical fantasy brought a wave of laughter from Meghan. She couldn't help but admire how he always embraced her quirks, how he was always ready to bring her fantasies to life. As she laughed, she realized this was one of the many reasons, why she loved Caleb – he was always ready to share in her dreams, no matter how whimsical they might be.

Unable to contain her laughter, Meghan ran towards Caleb, her heart filled with joy. She leaped into his arms, wrapping her arms around his neck as she looked up at him, her eyes twinkling with amusement and love. With a happy sigh, she leaned in, pressing her lips against his in a passionate kiss. Caleb, taken by surprise, held her tightly, returning her kiss with equal fervor.

As they shared their passionate kiss, they were both reminded of their deep love for each other. Their shared laughter, their shared dreams, their shared love – they were all reminders of the strong bond they shared. In that moment, they knew they were ready for whatever their future held – be it whatever was thrown their way. As long as they were together, they were ready to face anything that came their way.

Still holding Meghan in his arms, Caleb pulled away from their passionate kiss, his eyes twinkling with mischief. His lips curled into a playful smirk as he looked at Meghan, her cheeks still flushed from their kiss. "Hmm...I know what really turns you on now," he teased, his voice low and filled with mirth. The sight of Meghan blushing even more at his words brought another wave of laughter from him.

Meghan couldn't help but playfully swat at his chest, her laughter mingling with his. Despite her embarrassment, she couldn't deny that Caleb dressed as a cowboy was a sight she wouldn't mind seeing again. Their shared laughter and playful banter filled the air, a testament to their deep love and companionship.

The rest of the day was spent watching their favorite movies and sharing a delicious dinner. They talked about everything and nothing, their conversations flowing easily as they always did. As the day turned into night, they found themselves curled up on the couch, their bodies entwined as they shared stories, dreams, and laughter. Their shared warmth and the soft hum of their voices filled the room, creating a cozy and intimate atmosphere.

Eventually, their conversation slowed, their bodies growing heavy with exhaustion. As Caleb's eyes drifted shut, he pulled Meghan closer, his arms wrapping around her in a protective embrace. Meghan's head rested on his chest, her heart beating in sync with his. Slowly, they both succumbed to sleep, their bodies curled around each other in a comfortable tangle. As they slept, their dreams were filled with images of their shared future.

In the weeks that followed, Caleb busied himself with the wedding preparations. He reached out to caterers in Transylvania, researching and planning a traditional Transylvanian wedding feast. He wanted their wedding to be a unique blend of their personalities and cultures, a celebration that truly reflected their love story.

He spent hours on phone calls and emails, discussing menus, ingredients, and traditions. He learned about the local cuisine and the customs associated with weddings in Transylvania. He wanted everything to be perfect, a wedding feast that would not just satisfy their guests' palates but also give them a taste of the rich Transylvanian culture.

Meanwhile, Meghan supported him in every way she could, offering her inputs and helping him navigate through the planning process. Despite the stress and challenges, they found joy in planning their wedding together. Their shared dreams and goals brought them closer, strengthening their bond.

As they days passed, their excitement for their wedding grew. They could hardly wait for the day when they would finally say "I do" in the heart of Transylvania. Meghan was equally invested in the wedding preparations. She took care of the aesthetic details, ensuring that their wedding would be a visual feast. She arranged for an abundance of black and red roses, the colors symbolizing their passionate love and unyielding strength.

She also special ordered her wedding dress, changing the original black and purple design to black and red to match Calebs suit. She worked closely with the designer, explaining her vision and ensuring that every detail was perfect. The dress was a masterpiece, a stunning blend of elegance and boldness. The black fabric was adorned with intricate red patterns, the color catching the light and adding a touch of drama to the attire. It was a dress that reflected Meghan's personality – bold, unique, and beautiful.

As for Caleb's suit, it was a classic black design accentuated with red details and an added fur-topped cape that matched Meghan's dress. Together, they made a striking pair, their outfits a visual representation of their unique love story. As the wedding preparations were just about finished, the excitement was palpable. With every passing day, their dream of a life together was becoming more and more of a reality.

Deciding on a wedding date was their next step. As they sat down one evening, they found themselves filled with a mix of excitement and anticipation. After much discussion, they finally agreed on a date, marking the day on their calendar with a shared look of joy and excitement.

With the date finally set, they relayed the information to the wedding caterers, planners, and everyone else involved in their big day. Everything seemed to flow smoothly after that. The rental of Bran Castle was secured without a hitch, and the details of decorations and guest seating were meticulously planned out.

They spent their days going over the plans, making sure every detail was perfect. From the color of the tablecloths to the placement of the candles, everything was carefully considered. They wanted their wedding to be a reflection of their love story, a celebration that was uniquely them.

As they moved closer to their wedding day, their excitement grew. Every detail, every plan, brought them one step closer to their dream of a shared life. And as they navigated through the planning process, they found themselves falling in love all over again.

With the wedding date set for October 13th, they were in the final stretch of their preparations. The day held a special significance for them, not just because it was their wedding day, but also because it was a day that perfectly encapsulated their unique love story. The cool autumn weather, the spooky significance of the number 13, and the overall gothic aesthetic of their wedding venue were all elements that spoke volumes about their personalities and their relationship.

As they counted down the days, the excitement was palpable. They spent their days finalizing the last-minute details, ensuring everything was perfect for their big day. The caterers were ready, the castle was prepared, and their outfits were waiting.

Their evenings were spent in each other's arms, talking about their future, their dreams, and their goals. With every passing day, they found themselves falling deeper in love, their bond growing stronger. That night, as they lay in each other's arms, Caleb turned to face Meghan. His eyes were filled with excitement as he asked, "Meghan, are you ready to go to Romania?"

Meghan looked up at him, her eyes sparkling with anticipation. "And do some touring before our wedding day?", Caleb continued, his voice filled with hope. Meghan couldn't help the wide smile that spread across her face. The idea of exploring Romania before their wedding sounded wonderful. It was a chance to immerse themselves in the culture and familiarize themselves with their wedding venue.

"I would love that," Meghan replied, her voice filled with excitement. She could hardly wait to start this new adventure with Caleb. Whether it was exploring the beautiful landscapes of Romania or saying their vows in the heart of Transylvania, she knew that as long as they were together, they would create memories that would last a lifetime.

"There's one more thing we haven't really discussed yet," Caleb said, a teasing smile playing on his lips. Meghan looked at him, her eyes filled with curiosity. "What's that?" she asked, her heart fluttering with anticipation. Caleb's smile widened as he leaned in closer, his voice dropping to a whisper.

"Our honeymoon," he said, his eyes twinkling with mischief. Meghan's eyes widened in surprise, a blush creeping up her cheeks. In all their wedding preparations, they had completely forgotten about planning their honeymoon. A laugh bubbled up from Meghan's throat, her heart pounding with excitement. The thought of planning a honeymoon with Caleb filled her with joy. She could already imagine the endless possibilities – exploring exotic locations, cozying up in luxurious resorts, or even embarking on thrilling adventures.

"No matter where we go, I know it will be perfect," Meghan said, her voice filled with love. "As long as I'm with you, Caleb, every day feels like a honeymoon." Caleb's eyes softened at Meghan's words, his heart swelling with love for her. "I feel the same way, Meghan," he said, his voice tender. "Every moment with you is an adventure, and I look forward to spending the rest of my life with you."

He gently tucked a loose strand of hair behind her ear, his gaze never leaving hers. "We can discuss our honeymoon options tomorrow," he suggested. Meghan nodded, and her heart filled with anticipation for the adventure that awaited them. As they cuddled closer, their bodies tangled together in a comfortable embrace, they dreamed of their future.

Their journey to Romania marked the beginning of a new chapter in their lives, one they were eager to explore. As they drifted off to sleep, they were filled with excitement for the memories they were about to create, both in Romania and beyond.

The next morning, Caleb awoke before Meghan. He stretched, his gaze drifting to the sleeping form of his fiancée. A tender smile tugged at his lips as he watched her sleep, her features softened by the glow of the dimmed lights of the bedroom.

Quietly, he slipped out of their shared bed and headed towards the spacecraft's navigation room where he keyed in their destination. Caleb was surprised to realize that they weren't that far away from Romania. With the spacecraft's advanced technology, their journey would be relatively short, giving them plenty of time to explore Romania before their wedding day. A wave of anticipation washed over him. He could hardly wait to begin this new chapter of their lives.

After he set the navigation system to set the spacecraft down in a secluded area of Romania when they arrived, Caleb headed back to the bedroom where Meghan was still sleeping peacefully. A sense of warmth spread through him. He was about to embark on the greatest adventure of his life, and he had his best friend, his lover, his soon-to-be-wife by his side. With a happy sigh, he returned to their bed, deciding to let Meghan sleep a little longer. As he watched her sleep, he couldn't help but feel incredibly lucky. He was about to marry the love of his life in one of the most beautiful places on Earth. He couldn't ask for anything more.

About an hour later, Meghan stirred from her sleep, her eyes fluttering open to find Caleb sitting next to her. She sat up, stretching her arms above her head before laying her head on his shoulder. Her lips curled into a playful smirk as she nudged him lightly. "What, no breakfast yet?" she teased, her voice husky from sleep.

Caleb chuckled, turning to press a soft kiss to her forehead. "Well, someone decided to sleep in," he retorted playfully, his eyes twinkling with amusement. With a mock sigh, he climbed out of bed, stretching his arms above his head and got dressed. "Your wish is my command, my queen," he said, bowing dramatically before heading to the kitchen area of the spacecraft. Meghan laughed, shaking her head at his antics. Despite their teasing, they both knew how much they cherished these simple moments together.

As they started their day, they were reminded of just how much they loved each other – a love that was about to take them on the adventure of a lifetime. Meghan followed Caleb into the kitchen, a playful smile on her lips. As she approached him, she lightly smacked him on the ass, causing him to jump slightly, a surprise laugh escaping his lips.

"Can I help with breakfast?" she asked, her eyes twinkling with mischief. Caleb turned to face her, a grin spreading across his face. "I'd love that," he replied, his eyes warm. He pulled out a couple of ingredients from the fridge, setting them on the counter between them. As they set to work, the kitchen filled with the comforting scent of cooking food and the sound of their laughter. They worked seamlessly together, the easy banter, the shared glances. It was a reminder of their deep bond and the life they were about to build together.

As they sat down to eat, they shared stories, dreams and laughter, their love for each other as palpable as ever. And as they looked forward to their time in Romania and their upcoming wedding, they knew they were ready to face whatever came their way as long as they were together.

When their breakfast was finished and the table was cleared, Meghan looked at Caleb with a playful smile on her face. "Honeymoon options?" she asked, her eyes sparkling with excitement. Before Caleb could respond, Meghan quickly added, "And don't say you're good with wherever I want to go. I want to know where YOU would like to go."

Caleb stared at her, a slow smile spreading on his face. He loved how Meghan always made sure he had a say in their plans, how she valued his opinions and desires. "Well," he started, his eyes twinkling with excitement, "I've always wanted to explore the beaches of the Maldives. The clear turquoise waters, the white sandy beaches...it seems like a paradise. "But," he quickly added, looking at Meghan, "I also know you love history and architecture. So, maybe a tour across Europe? Visiting the ancient cities, exploring the historic sites...what do you think?"

He looked at Meghan, his eyes filled with anticipation, eager to hear her thoughts, and ready to plan their dream honeymoon together. Meghan smiled, "Maldives sounds wonderful!" Caleb's face broke into a wide grin as Meghan's words sank in. "Maldives it is then," he said, his voice filled with excitement. He could already picture it – the clear blue waters, the white sandy beaches, and most importantly, Meghan by his side.

He reached out, taking Meghan's hand in his. "Maldives will be perfect. Just like us," he said, his gaze softening as he looked at her. He could hardly wait to start this new adventure with Meghan. As they sat there, hand in hand, their hearts filled with anticipation, they knew that their honeymoon in the Maldives was going to be another beautiful chapter in their incredible love story.

As Meghan got up from the table, Caleb watched her, his eyes filled with love. She walked around the table and came up behind him, leaning over his shoulder and wrapping her arms around him. The warmth of her body against his sent a thrill through him, making his heart flutter.

She nibbled at his ear, sending shivers down his spine. Then, she kissed the side of his chin, her lips brushing against his stubble. It was a simple, intimate gesture that filled him with happiness. "I love you more than ever," she whispered into his ear, her voice filled with emotion. Caleb turned in her arms, his hands coming up to cup her face. He looked into her eyes, seeing the depth of her love for him.

"And I love you," he replied, his voice barely above a whisper. He leaned in, capturing her lips in a sweet, lingering kiss. It was a promise, a vow of his eternal love for her. A love that was about to take them on an unforgettable journey, from their wedding in Romania to their honeymoon in the Maldives.

Meghan straddled Caleb's lap, her arms winding around his neck, his heart fluttered in his chest. Her proximity, the intimacy of their position, sent a thrill coursing through him. Her question brought him back to the present. "So, what are we doing today while we travel across the sky in this luxury spacecraft?" Her voice was teasing, her eyes sparkling with excitement.

Caleb grinned, his hands coming to rest on her waist. "Well," he said, his voice low, "we could check out the observation deck, maybe. The views of Earth from up here are breathtaking, or," he continued, his eyes twinkling with mischief, "we could watch some movies, play some games...or just enjoy each other's company."

He leaned in, pressing a soft kiss to her lips. "Whatever we do, I know it will be perfect, because I'll be with you." Meghan smiles, "You haven't shown me the observation deck yet." Caleb's eyes lit up at Meghan's words. "You're in for a treat," he said, his voice filled with excitement. The observation deck was one of his favorite parts of the spacecraft. It offered stunning views of Earth and the vast expanse of space.

He gently helped Meghan up off his lap and took her hand in his. "Come on, let's go," he said, leading her towards the observation deck. As they stepped onto the deck, Caleb watched Meghan's reaction closely. The sight that greeted them was breathtaking – the Earth, a beautiful blue and green sphere, against the backdrop of the infinite blackness of space, speckled with countless stars.

He looked at Meghan, his heart swelling with love for her. This was just the start of their journey, and he couldn't wait to explore the rest of the universe with her. Meghan's gasp echoed through the silent observation deck as she took in the incredible view. Her hand instinctively tightened around Caleb's as she stared out at the earth, the vibrant blues and greens of the planet stark against the inky blackness of space.

"It's…it's beautiful," she breathed out, her voice full of awe. She turned to look at Caleb, her eyes shining with excitement. "I never imagined it would be this…breathtaking." Caleb grinned, feeling a sense of pride. He loved that he could share this with her, that they were able to experience such beauty together. "It's one of the many perks of space travel," he said, his arm slipping around her waist to pull her closer.

They stood there for what felt like hours, just watching the earth slowly rotate, the countries and oceans passing by beneath them. It was a moment of peace, a moment of shared wonder that they would remember for the rest of their lives.

Breaking the comfortable silence that had settled between them, Meghan turned to Caleb, her eyes filled with curiosity. "When will we land in Romania?" she asked, her voice echoing slightly in the spacious deck. Caleb glanced at his wristwatch, a thoughtful look on his face. "With our current speed, we should be landing in about three hours," he replied, his gaze meeting hers.

He squeezed her hand gently, excitement bubbling up within him. "Are you excited?" he asked, his voice filled with anticipation. The idea of landing in Romania, of starting this new chapter of their lives, filled him with a sense of joy and anticipation he couldn't quite put into words.

As they stood there, the Earth spinning slowly beneath them, they couldn't help but feel incredibly lucky. Meghan smiles, "Yes, I am very excited!" Caleb couldn't help but return Meghan's smile, her excitement infectious. "I'm glad," he said sincerely, his thumb gently stroking the back of her hand. "This is going to be an adventure like no other." With a shared smile and a sense of adventure in their hearts, they turned to look back at the Earth one last time before heading back to their quarters, ready for the journey ahead.

Meghan turns to Caleb and asks, "Will anyone from your family be coming to our wedding?" As Meghan brought up his family, Caleb tensed, his jovial mood evaporating instantly. He turned away from her, his gaze fixed elsewhere. He didn't know how to tell her about his five brothers, how they despised everything about Earth and had disowned him for falling in love with an Earthling.

Meghan's happiness and excitement about their upcoming wedding and honeymoon was infectious, and the last thing he wanted to do was bring her down with his family drama. He took a deep breath, steeling himself for the conversation. "My family…they won't be coming to the wedding," he said finally, his voice barely above a whisper. He turned to look at her, his eyes filled with a mixture of sadness and determination. "And I'd rather not talk about them anymore."

He didn't want his family's negativity to cast a shadow over their happiness. He wanted to focus on his future with Meghan, on their life together, not on his past and the family that had rejected the idea of his soulmate being not of their world. Meghan takes Caleb's hands in hers, "I don't know what has happened within your family, but if you ever want to talk, I will always be here for you, no matter what."

Meghan's words brought a sense of relief to Caleb, the weight of his family's rejection lifting slightly. He turned to look at her, gratitude shining in his eyes. "Thank you," he said softly, his voice filled with emotion. He reached out, pulling her into a tight embrace, his arms wrapping around her. Her understanding and support meant the world to him in that moment. He held her close, feeling comforted by her presence. "I appreciate your understanding more than you know." He pressed a gentle kiss to her forehead, expressing his gratitude in a silent gesture.

He knew that Meghan meant every word she said, and that thought brought him a sense of peace. He knew that no matter what challenges or difficulties they faced, they would always have each other for support and comfort. And that, to him, was everything.

As the weight of their respective family situations hung in the air, Caleb shifted the conversation to Meghan's family. He wanted to show her that he was there for her too, that they could share their burdens and joys together.

"Meghan, tell me about your family," Caleb said gently, his voiced filled with warmth and compassion. Meghan hesitated for a moment, unsure of how to broach the topic. Finally, she took a deep breath and met Caleb's gaze. "I...I don't have any siblings," she started, her voice soft. "And my parents passed away a few years ago in a vehicle accident."

She looked down, unable to meet Caleb's eyes, unsure of how he would react to her painful past. The loss of her parents still weighed heavily on her heart, and she wondered if Caleb would understand her pain.

Caleb's heart ached for Meghan as she shared her story. He reached out, taking her hands in his, offering her comfort and support. "I'm so sorry, Meghan," he said, his voice filled with empathy. "I can't imagine how difficult that must have been for you."

He pulled her into a comforting embrace, holding her close. In that moment, they found solace in each other's arms, sharing their burdens and sorrows, knowing that they were not alone in their pain. And as they stood there, united in their grief and their love for each other, they knew that no matter what life threw at them, they would face it together, hand in hand.

As Caleb held Meghan close, he couldn't shake the weight of the secret he carried about his family. He knew that eventually he would have to tell Meghan more about his siblings and the complicated dynamics that existed within his family. But for now, he wanted to protect her from the potential danger and turmoil that his siblings could bring.

Caleb was the oldest of his parents' brood, and with that came a certain level of responsibility and power over his five siblings. He knew that they might not take kindly to his relationship with Meghan, especially given their disdain for Earth and Earthlings. He feared that they might try to come after Meghan, and he was determined to shield her from any potential harm.

For now, Caleb chose to keep his family secrets to himself, not wanting to scare Meghan or burden her with his family's troubles. He knew that when the time came, he would have to be honest with her, but for now, he wanted to focus on their love and their future together.

As they stood there, wrapped in each other's arms, Caleb made a silent vow to protect Meghan at all costs, to shield her from any harm that might come their way. And as they shared a moment of quiet understanding and love, he knew that no matter what challenges they faced, they would face them together, united in their love and their commitment to each other.

Chapter 5

The spacecraft settled gently into a secluded forest in Romania, the invisibility cloak activating automatically to shield the vehicle from prying eyes. The hum of the engines slowly died down, leaving them in the quiet serenity of the Romanian wilderness.

Turning to look at Meghan, Caleb saw the same excitement mirrored in her eyes that he felt coursing through his veins. "Are you ready to go exploring Romania tomorrow?" he asked, his voice filled with anticipation. Meghan's eye lit up at the prospect. "Absolutely," she replied, her voice steady and filled with excitement. "I can't wait to see everything Romania has to offer."

Caleb felt a thrill of anticipation as he thought about the adventures that awaited them. Whether it was exploring the rich history and culture of Romania, or simply spending time together in this new and exciting place, he knew that this was only the beginning of their incredible journey together.

As they settled into their quarters for the night, the excitement of their upcoming adventures made sleep elusive. But eventually, they drifted off to sleep, dreaming of the adventures that awaited them in Romania.

A sudden chill ran down Caleb's spine, pulling him from a deep sleep. Something was off, he could sense it. With a glance at Meghan, peacefully asleep beside him, he carefully slipped out of bed so as not to disturb her. He quickly dressed in the dim light, his movements quiet and efficient. He didn't know what was wrong, but he had learned to trust his instincts over the years. Especially when it came to matters that could potentially endanger him or those he cared about.

Once dressed, he made his way to the control panel of the spacecraft. He began to scan the immediate area for any signs of trouble, his eyes darting over the various screens and data. Everything seemed quiet and normal, but Caleb couldn't shake the feeling in unease. He decided to do a quick perimeter check around the spacecraft, just to be sure. He didn't want to take any chances, especially not when Meghan's safety was at stake.

As he moved silently through the dark forest, Caleb was alert to any sounds or movements. He hoped that his instincts were wrong this time, but he knew better than to ignore them. The sudden appearance of a dark figure stepping out from behind a tree sent Caleb's senses into high alert. The familiar voice that echoed around him made his heart drop.

"Well, well, hello big brother," the figure said, his voice laced with a chilling hint of amusement. "Brett," Caleb said, his voice steady despite the surprise. He hadn't expected any of his brothers to find him, especially not this soon. He had hoped for more time to prepare, to figure out how to handle this situation.

Brett's silhouette moved closer, his form becoming more defined under the moonlight. "Never thought I'd find you here, Caleb. On Earth, of all places," he said, his voice filled with disdain. Caleb stood his ground, his mind racing. He needed to keep Brett away from Meghan and the spacecraft. He needed to figure out why Brett was here and what he wanted, as if he didn't already know.

But for now, he had to play it cool. "What brings you to Earth, Brett?" he asked, trying to keep his voice casual. He hoped that his surprise visit didn't spell trouble for him and Meghan. Brett's words sent a chill down Caleb's spine, confirming his worst fears. His brother was here because of Meghan, and his intentions were far from friendly.

"You didn't really think I was about to let you get away with marrying a despicable little piece of shit earthling, did you?!" Brett said, a cruel smile playing on his lips. Caleb felt a surge of anger at his brother's words. Meghan was anything but 'despicable'. She was kind, brave, and everything he could ever ask for.

"What are you going to do, Brett?" Caleb asked, trying to keep his voice steady. He refused to let his brother's cruel words get to him. He would protect Meghan, no matter what. Brett's smile widened, but he didn't respond immediately. He seemed to be enjoying the tension, the uncertainty. Caleb knew he had to act fast, to get back to Meghan before Brett could cause any harm. But he also knew that he had to tread carefully. Any rash action could escalate the situation, and that was the last thing he wanted.

Caleb forced himself to remain calm, despite the rage boiling within him at his brother's words. "You need to leave, Brett," he said, his voice firm. Brett laughed, a cruel, harsh sound that echoed through the quiet forest. "Does she even know what you are?!" he sneered. "How, Caleb, could you even fathom loving something so vile as an earthling?!"

Caleb clenched his fists at his sides, his anger flaring. But he knew he couldn't let Brett provoke him. He needed to stay calm, for Meghan's sake. "Meghan is worth more than you'll ever understand," he retorted, his voice steady. "And yes, she knows who I am, and she loves me. Now, I'm going to ask you one last time. Leave. Now."

Caleb stood his ground, staring down his brother. He hoped his words would be enough to send Brett away. But if they weren't, he would do whatever it took to protect Meghan. He loved her, and he would not let Brett or anyone else harm her.

As Brett stepped closer, uttering his vile threat, Caleb's instincts kicked in. Fear for Meghan's safety, combined with a surge of adrenaline, propelled him into action. In a swift, almost imperceptible movement, Caleb reached into his boot, pulling out a small, deadly poisonous dagger. Before Brett could react, Caleb lunged, his hand closing around his brother's throat. He plunged the dagger into Brett's side, the poison instantly coursing through his veins.

Brett's eyes widened in shock before his body went limp, the life draining from him almost instantly. Caleb let go, Brett's lifeless body collapsing onto the forest floor. Caleb stood over his brother, his breathing heavy, his heart pounding in his chest. He felt a pang of sorrow for what he had done, but he knew he had no other choice.

He quickly turned and sprinted back to the spacecraft, praying that Meghan was still safe. He couldn't shake the feeling of dread that had settled in his stomach. He had dealt with one threat, but he knew there were more out there. His brothers wouldn't stop until they got what they wanted. But neither would he. He would do anything to protect Meghan, his love, his life.

Before reentering the spacecraft, Caleb paused, glancing back at Brett's lifeless body. He couldn't leave him there, not when there was a risk that his presence could draw unwanted attention. With a heavy sigh, Caleb extended his hand, concentrating on the familiar sensation of his teleportation power. A bright light enveloped Brett's body, and within seconds, it disappeared, sent into oblivion.

Caleb felt a pang of regret and sorrow for his brother. Despite everything, they were still family. But he knew he had done what he needed to do to protect Meghan. With Brett's body taken care of, Caleb turned back to the spacecraft. His heart pounded in his chest as he hurried inside, desperate to ensure Meghan was safe. This night had taken a dark turn, and he knew that things were only going to get more complicated from here. But no matter what, he would face it head-on, for Meghan's sake.

As Caleb reentered their bedroom, he was relieved to find Meghan still asleep, oblivious to the chaos that had unfolded outside. He watched he for a moment, her face peaceful in sleep, and his heart ached with the love he felt for her. Quietly, he knelt down beside the bed, his mind racing with thoughts. He knew he couldn't keep the truth from Meghan any longer. She deserved to know about his brothers, about the potential danger they were in.

He watched Meghan sleep, her chest rising and falling rhythmically, and wished he could protect her from the harsh reality of his world. But he knew he had to tell her. She had a right to know and prepare herself.

Taking a deep breath, Caleb reached out, gently brushing a stray lock of hair from Meghan's face. "Meghan, I need to tell you something," he began, his voice soft but filled with sincerity. He would tell her everything, and whatever happened next, they would face together.

As Caleb gently woke her, Meghan opened her eyes slowly, sleep still clinging to them. "Caleb?" she mumbled; her voice thick with sleep. When she saw the look in his eyes though, she snapped to attention. His usually warm and confident gaze was filled with fear and something that looked like regret. She reached out, placing a hand on his arm, her heart pounding in her chest. "What's wrong?" she asked, her voice steady despite the worry that welled up inside her.

Caleb took a deep breath, mentally preparing himself to tell her everything. He had to be honest with her, even if the truth, to understand the danger they were in. And he would do whatever it took to keep her safe, no matter what.

Taking a deep breath, Caleb began to explain. He told Meghan about Brett, about their confrontation in the woods and the deadly outcome. He explained the potential threat from his other four brothers, their dislike for Earth and Earthlings, and their potential to pose a real danger to them. As he spoke, Caleb kept his eyes on Meghan, watching her closely for any signs of fear or panic. He knew this was a lot to take in and he braced himself for her reaction.

Meghan was silent for a long moment after Caleb finished speaking, her eyes wide and filled with disbelief. Caleb could see her mind working, processing the information he had just revealed. He knew this was a lot for her to take in, but he also knew that she was strong. He hoped that their love was strong enough to withstand this.

Finally, Meghan spoke. Her voice was soft, but there was a steeliness to it that made Caleb's heart swell with love and admiration. "We'll face them together, Caleb," she said firmly. "We won't let them tear us apart."

As he looked into Meghan's determined eyes, Caleb knew they could face anything together. They were stronger together, and with their love, they could overcome anything.

Meghan reached out, her hand gently cupping Caleb's cheek. The look in her eyes was one of complete trust, a depth of emotion that took Caleb's breath away. "Caleb," she said softly, her gaze never leaving his. "I trust you. Completely. I know you will keep me safe."

The sincerity in her voice, the absolute faith she had in him, it was humbling. Caleb felt a lump form in his throat, his heart swelling with love for Meghan. He knew in that moment that he would do anything, face any danger, to keep her safe.

He covered her hand with his, pressing a gentle kiss to her palm. "I will always protect you, Meghan. I promise," he vowed, his voice choked with emotion. He would face his brothers, face any danger that came their way, to keep Meghan safe. Because he loved her more than anything in the universe, and he would do whatever it took to protect her.

Meghan's smile was like the dawn after a long night, warming Caleb's heart and bringing light to the shadows of his fears. She slid off the bed and into his lap, her arms winding around his neck. Their bodies fit together perfectly, as if they were two pieces of a puzzle that had finally found their match.

"I love you, Caleb," she whispered, her voice filled with a warmth that made his heart flutter. "Nothing or no one could ever change that." Caleb felt a rush of emotion, his heart pounding in his chest. He pulled her closer, his arms wrapping around her in a tight embrace. He buried his face in her hair, inhaling the sweet scent of her. She was his safe haven, his anchor in the storm.

"I love you too, Meghan," he murmured, his voice barely above a whisper. He pulled back slightly, his gaze meeting hers. He leaned in, capturing her lips in a tender kiss, a promise of his unwavering love and protection.

As they sat there, wrapped in each other's arms, Caleb knew they could face anything together. No matter what threats his brothers posed, they would overcome it together. Their love was stronger than any danger, stronger than any fear. And nothing could ever change that.

Gently, Meghan untangled herself from Caleb's embrace and stood up. She extended her hand towards him, pulling him up as well. Their eyes met, and they shared a quiet, intimate moment, acknowledging the journey they were about to embark on together. As one, they climbed back into bed, their bodies instinctively seeking the comfort of each other's presence. Caleb wrapped his arms around Meghan, pulling her close against him. His heart pounded in his chest at the feel of her, the steady rhythm of her breathing a comforting presence.

He pressed his lips to her forehead, a silent promise of his love and protection. Meghan snuggled closer into his embrace, her sigh of contentment echoing in the quiet room. Their love was their greatest weapon, their strongest shield. And together, they were invincible.

The morning light streamed through the window, casting a golden glow over the room. Caleb stirred; his arms still wrapped around Meghan. He pressed a soft kiss to her forehead, causing her to stir. Her eyes fluttered open, meeting his. "Good morning, love," he greeted her with a soft smile. Meghan returned his smile, snuggling closer into his arms. "Morning," she murmured, her voice still thick with sleep.

After a moment, Caleb pulled back slightly, his gaze serious. "Meghan," he began, "are you ready to explore Romania?" Meghan looked at him, her eyes sparkling with excitement. "Yes, I'm ready!"

As they rose from the bed and began to get dressed, Caleb couldn't help the worry that crept into his thoughts. His confrontation with Brett was still fresh in his mind, and he couldn't shake the feeling of unease. He knew his brothers were less likely to show up during broad daylight, but he also knew that they were unpredictable. And after what happened with Brett, he wasn't willing to take any chances. As he slipped on his jacket, his hand brushed against the hilt of the blade he had tucked inside. It was a small comfort, but it was enough. He was ready, prepared to protect Meghan at any cost.

Caleb looked over at Meghan, her face glowing with excitement as she pulled on her boots. He couldn't help but smile at her enthusiasm, her spirit. She was his light in the darkness, his strength in the face of adversity.

With a final glance around the room, Caleb extended his hand towards Meghan. "Let's go," he said, his voice filled with determination. They had a long day ahead of them, and he was ready to face whatever came their way. Together.

With a firm grip on Meghan's hand, Caleb focused his mind, the familiar sensation of teleportation washing over him. In an instant, they were gone, leaving the safety of their spacecraft behind. When they reappeared, they were in the heart of Transylvania. The air was cool and crisp, the early morning light casting long shadows over the cobblestone streets. The architecture was a rich blend of old and new, presenting a scene that was both beautiful and slightly eerie.

Caleb looked around, taking in the sights and sounds of the city. I was bustling with activity, even at this early hour. He turned to Meghan; her eyes wide with wonder as she took in their surroundings. "Let's find a place for breakfast," he suggested, giving her hand a reassuring squeeze. They needed to keep their strength up, especially if they were going to be exploring all day.

Meghan nodded; her excitement palpable. "Sounds like a plan," she agreed, her eyes sparkling with anticipation. She looked up at Caleb, her gaze filled with trust and love. It was a moment that warmed Caleb's heart, giving him the strength he needed to face whatever lay ahead.

As they strolled down the streets, a particular place caught Caleb's eye. A quaint café called 'Galeria Bran', with its inviting exterior and the delicious aroma of fresh bread wafting out. He pointed it out to Meghan, asking, "What about this place here for breakfast?" Meghan looked up at the café, a smile spreading on her face. "It looks cozy," she replied, her hand squeezing his. "Let's try it."

With a nod, Caleb led them towards the café, his hand firmly holding Meghan's. Despite the potential threat of his brothers, the morning felt surprisingly normal, almost peaceful. They were just two people in love, exploring a new city together, and for a moment, Caleb allowed himself to enjoy it.

As they stepped into the café, the warm, cozy atmosphere enveloped them. The mouth-watering smell of freshly baked bread and brewing coffee filled the air, making Meghan's eyes light up with delight. Caleb couldn't help but smile at her excitement. Despite the threats and the danger, moments like these made everything worth it.

They were escorted to a snug corner table, bathed in the soft morning light filtering through a nearby window. The café was alive with the hum of activity, the sounds of clinking silverware, hushed conversation, and the irresistible scent of food permeating the air.

The waitress, a jovial woman with a warm smile, handed them two menus. "Luati-va timp," she said in fluent Romanian, which meant 'take your time', before she bustled off to cater to another table.

Caleb shared a glance with Meghan, a gentle smile resting on his lips. As his gaze wondered over the menu, the options were varied, featuring traditional Romanian fare to more universally recognized comfort food. Meghan's eyes shimmered with anticipation as she skimmed through her menu. "Everything looks so delicious," she mused, her gaze bouncing between the menu and Caleb. "I can't decide where to begin."

Meghan looked at Caleb with a blushed smile, "Caleb, do you speak Romanian?" Caleb grinned back at her, nodding his head. "Yes, babe, I do. Would you like me to order for you?" he offered, already studying the menu with a thoughtful expression. Meghan's smile widened and she nodded, her eyes sparkling with amusement and admiration. "Yes, would you please?" she responded her hand squeezing his. Caleb chuckled lightly, his gaze still on the menu. "Alright," he said, already deciding on a few dishes he thought she would enjoy.

When the waitress returned to their table, she queried in Romanian, "Ce pot sa va aduc in aceasta dimineata?" which meant 'what can I get for you this morning?' Caleb, speaking fluently in Romanian answered, "Pentru mine, o omleta cu sunca si branza si suc de portocale, va rog. Si pentru ea, o omleta cu legume si branza si suc de portocale." This translated to 'For me, a ham and cheese omelet and orange juice, please. And for her, a vegetable and cheese omelet and orange juice.' The waitress nodded, scribbling down their order before giving them a smile and heading back towards the kitchen. Caleb turned back to Meghan, his eyes sparkling with amusement as he waited her reaction.

Meghan's cheeks flushed a soft pink as she smiled at Caleb. "How do you know so many languages?" she asked, her eyes wide with curiosity and admiration. Caleb couldn't help but grin at her reaction, "Oh, do you forget who I am and where I'm from?" he teased, his voice light. "I can speak any language that I need to."

His playful response drew a soft laugh from Meghan, her smile widening. She shook her head at him, her eyes sparkling with love. "You never cease to amaze me, Caleb," she said, reaching across the table to hold his hand.

Just moments later, the waitress returned, balancing two plates and a pair of glasses on her tray. The aroma of the freshly prepared omelets wafted through the air, making their stomachs growl in anticipation. With a cheerful, "Pofta buna!", which meant 'Enjoy your meal', she set down their breakfast. Meghan's vegetable and cheese omelet was a fluffy delight, garnished with fresh herbs. Caleb's ham and cheese omelet looked equally appetizing; the cheese melted to perfection. The glasses of orange juice were chilled, the citrusy aroma refreshing.

They shared a grateful smile with the waitress before she moved on to attend to her other customers. As they started their breakfast, the flavors were as wonderful as the aroma had promised, making them hum in delight.

After breakfast, Caleb and Meghan spent the rest of the morning exploring the local shops. The streets were lined with quaint storefronts, each one offering unique treasures. From handcrafted jewelry to vintage books, every shop held something new and exciting.

Caleb, ever the doting partner, insisted on buying everything that Meghan showed an interest in. A delicate necklace here, a beautifully bound book there. Despite her protests, he would simply smile and hand over his credit chip, his eyes twinkling with affection. But Meghan didn't care for material things. Sure, it was nice to have them, but they weren't what mattered the most to her. What she truly desired, what she truly valued, was spending time with Caleb. Sharing adventures with him, creating memories – that was what mattered to her. That was what she really wanted.

As they walked hand in hand through the bustling streets of Transylvania, Meghan knew that she was exactly where she wanted to be. With Caleb by her side, she was ready to face any challenge, ready to embark on any adventure. To her, it wasn't about the destination. It was about the journey, and more importantly, the person she was sharing it with. Caleb was her partner, her love, her everything.

As lunchtime approached, Caleb teleported them back to the safety of their spacecraft. The items he had bought Meghan during their exploration were already there, having been transported separately.

In the familiar confines of their spacecraft, they fixed a simple lunch for themselves. As they worked side by side, they chatted about everything they had seen so far. The stunning architecture, the quaint shops, the friendly locals – every experience was a new memory they were creating together.

Meghan couldn't help but laugh as Caleb mimicked the way one of the shopkeepers had spoken, his impression spot-on. Caleb grinned at her laughter, his heart swelling with love for her. These simple moments, these shared experiences – they were what made everything worth it.

As they sat down to eat, they continued their conversation, their laughter filling the spacecraft. Despite the dangers they faced, despite the looming threat of Caleb's brothers, they were content.

As evening descended, Caleb and Meghan decided to stay in the relative safety of their spacecraft. The day had been long and filled with excitement, and they both agreed that a quiet evening was just what they needed. As they settled into the comfortable seating area, Meghan turned to Caleb, her eyes sparkling with anticipation. "Caleb, can we tour some of the castles tomorrow morning?" she asked, her excitement palpable.

Caleb couldn't help but smile at her enthusiasm. "Of course we can, babe," he assured her, his own curiosity piqued. "Those old castles have been around for a very long time. I'm curious to see the inside décor." Meghan grinned at his agreement, her heart fluttering in anticipation. She loved exploring new places, especially ones rich in history and culture like the castles. And getting to do it with Caleb made it even more special.

As they settled in for the evening, their minds were filled with thoughts of the adventures that awaited them the next day. Meghan's gaze softened as she looked at Caleb, her heart full of love for him. "Our wedding is only a week away," she said, her voice filled with anticipation and joy. "I can't wait to be your wife."

Caleb's heart swelled at her words, his eyes mirroring her affection. "And I can't wait to call you my wife," he responded earnestly, reaching out to take her hand in his. Their impending wedding added another layer of excitement and anticipation to their adventure.

As they settled in for the night, their hearts were filled with love and anticipation for the future. They had a week of adventures and challenges ahead of them, but they also had something even more exciting to look forward to – their wedding.

As the veil of night enshrouded the spacecraft, Caleb lay awake for a few moments longer, simply watching Meghan. She had drifted off to sleep beside him, her head nestled comfortably against his bare chest, her hand resting over his heart. Her steady breathing was a soothing rhythm, lulling him towards sleep. But for a moment, he resisted the pull of slumber, choosing instead to bask in the utter contentment that filled him. He felt like the luckiest being alive. To have Meghan by his side, to share these moments of tranquility amidst the chaos, it felt like a dream. A dream he never wanted to awaken from.

Caleb traced a gentle finger over Meghan's hand, his gaze softening as he watched her sleep. Love swelled within him; a feeling so profound it left him breathless. He knew then, he would do anything to protect her, to ensure she remained safe and happy. With a soft sigh, he tightened his hold on her just a fraction, pulling her even closer against him. His eyes fluttered closed as he finally gave in to sleep, his last thoughts filled with Meghan and the love they shared.

Over the next few days, Caleb and Meghan spent their time touring the grand castles of Transylvania. Each one was a piece of history, a testament to the ages past. The architecture was exquisite, the interiors filled with vintage art and décor that spoke of a time long gone.

One of the castles they visited was Bran Castle, most famously known as Dracula's Castle. Despite the chilling legends surrounding it, the castle was a stunning piece of architecture, its towering structure standing proudly against the backdrop of the Carpathian Mountains. They spent hours exploring the castle, marveling at the vintage décor and learning about the history.

As they walked through the grand halls and the winding staircases, they couldn't help but admire the beauty and mystery of the place. But what made Bran Castle extra special was the fact that it was going to be the venue for their wedding. As they stood in the grand hall, where their ceremony would take place, they could almost picture it. The hall filled with their guests, the air filled with joy and celebration, and them standing at the altar, pledging their love for each other.

The thought brought a smile to their faces, a sense of anticipation and excitement filling them. Despite the challenges they faced, they couldn't wait for their wedding day. It was going to be a day of love, joy, and celebration.

The following day was dedicated to finalizing the wedding preparations. Caleb and Meghan met with the wedding caterers and planners at Bran Castle, going over the last-minute details. They tasted and approved the menu, a delightful array of local delicacies and international favorites. They approved the floral arrangements, the color scheme, and the layout of the ceremony and reception.

When the subject of the guest list came up, Caleb addressed it with a smile. "We do not have family that will be attending the wedding," he said, his gaze meeting Meghan's for a moment before continuing. "But we would like to invite the locals of Transylvania. They are more than welcome to attend our wedding and the feast afterwards.

The planners and caterers nodded, making a note of it. It was an unusual request, but then again, this was an unusual wedding. The bride and groom were foreigners, the venue was Dracula's Castle, and now, the entire local population was invited. But the excitement in their eyes was infectious, and everyone involved in the planning found themselves looking forward to the big day.

As Caleb and Meghan left the castle that day, their hearts were filled with anticipation. Their wedding was the very next day, and they couldn't wait to celebrate their love with the locals of Transylvania. It was going to be a day to remember, a day filled with love and joy.

The following morning arrived with a sense of anticipation and excitement. As the first rays of sunlight bathed Transylvania, Caleb and Meghan were already up and heading to Bran Castle for their wedding. In separate rooms, they prepared for their special day. Meghan slipped into her black and red wedding gown, a stunning piece that accentuated her beauty. The dress was a perfect blend of traditional and modern, much like their love story.

In another room, Caleb donned a matching black and red suit, looking every bit the handsome groom. Despite the nerves that fluttered in his stomach, he couldn't help but smile. Today, he was marrying the love of his life.

A few minutes later, Caleb was shown where to stand. As he looked around, he was touched by the number of locals who had come to share this special day with him and Meghan. Their presence warmed his heart, their smiles and well-wishes making the day even more special.

As the music began to play, all eyes turned towards the entrance. And then, there she was. Meghan, looking radiant and beautiful, was walking down the aisle towards him. Caleb's breath hitched in his throat as he watched her, his heart pounding with love and adoration. This was it. Their special day had finally arrived. And as Meghan walked towards him, Caleb knew that he was the luckiest being in the universe. Because he was about to marry the woman he loved more than anything in his life.

When Meghan finally reached Caleb, the minister began the ceremony. Their surroundings faded into a blur as they focused solely on each other, their hearts brimming with love and anticipation. When the time came for their vows, they chose to recite their own. Meghan went first, her voice clear and steady as she held Caleb's hands. Her eyes, filled with love, never left his as she began her vow.

"I'm madly in love with you," she began, her voice filled with emotion. "Not only do I promise that my love will grow with each day, but I promise to be your friend and partner every step of the way. I will be there for you, day or night, in richer or poorer, in sickness and in health." She paused for a moment, her grip tightening around Caleb's hands. "I trust, appreciate, cherish, and respect you. I promise to share with you my hopes and dreams as we build our lives together. Caleb, I give you this ring as my promise to you. You, my love, are my everything."

Her words hung in the air, a tangible testament of her love for Caleb. They were heartfelt and sincere, promising a lifetime of love and companionship. With Meghan's vows still echoing in his heart, Caleb now took his turn to express his love and commitment. His voice was firm and filled with emotion as he began his vows.

"Do you remember the very first day that we met?" he started, his gaze locked onto Meghan's. "I knew the very first moment I saw you. I knew we were meant to be together for all eternity." He paused for a moment, his grip on Meghan's hands tightening. "You have become my lover, my companion, and my best friend. There's no one else I'd want to build a life with," he continued, his voice thick with emotion. A tender smile graced his lips as he concluded his vows. Meghan, I give you this ring as my promise to you. I get to have you by my side, my love and my wife, for eternity."

His words were heartfelt and sincere, a promise of a lifetime of love and togetherness. As he finished, the crowd erupted into applause, their cheers ringing throughout the grand hall. Their vows were a testament to their love, a promise of a future filled with love and companionship. And as they stood there, hand in hand, they knew that they were ready to face whatever the future held, together.

As the minister concluded the ceremony, a sense of joy and love filled the air. The moment they had been waiting for had finally arrived. "I now pronounce you man and wife," the minister declared, his words resonating through the grand hall of Bran Castle. "Caleb, you may kiss your bride."

Caleb's heart swelled with love and happiness as he looked into Meghan's eyes. Without hesitation, he gently lifted her veil, his hands cradling her face as he leaned in towards Meghan, his heart brimming with love and joy. Closing the distance between them, he pressed his lips to hers in a tender and passionate kiss. Time seemed to stand still as they shared this first kiss as husband and wife, sealing their vows and promised to each other.

As they finally pulled away, their eyes met, filled with a shared love and a promise of a future together. Hand in hand, they turned to face their guests, ready to embark on the next chapter of their lives as husband and wife.

As the minister's words rang out, declaring them as Mr. and Mrs. Caleb Stozick, a wave joy washed over the newlyweds. Caleb and Meghan exchanged a loving glance, their hearts full of happiness and gratitude for this moment.

The crowd erupted into cheers and applause, their joyous celebration echoing through the grand hall of Bran Castle. Caleb and Meghan held each other close, savoring the moment of pure happiness and love. With intertwined hands, they walked back down the aisle as husband and wife, their steps light and their smiles radiant. The guests, caught up in the spirit of celebration, showered them with red and black rose petals, their cheers and well wishes filling the air.

The petals fluttered around Caleb and Meghan like a cascade of blessings, each one a symbol of love, happiness, and good fortune for their new life together. They walked through the shower of petals, feeling the warmth and love of their guests surrounding them, blessing them with all the best that life had to offer.

Hand in hand, Caleb and Meghan emerged from the castle, ready to embark on their journey together as husband and wife, their hearts united in love and their future shining bright with promise. The echoes of the cheers and the fragrances of the petals lingered in the air, a beautiful reminder of the love and joy that filled their special day.

As Caleb and Meghan entered the area set up for their wedding reception, a mouthwatering aroma filled the air. The scent of traditional Romanian delicacies wafted around them, tempting their taste buds and adding to the festive atmosphere of the celebration. Long tables were adorned with colorful tablecloths, and floral centerpieces, and the guests were seated, eagerly awaiting the arrival of the newlyweds. The sound of lively music played in the background, setting the tone for a joyous celebration.

But what caught Caleb and Meghan's attention the most was the wedding cake. Towering in the center of the room, the cake was a masterpiece in the shape of Bran Castle itself. Every intricate detail of the castle was recreated in sugary perfection, from the turrets to the gates, capturing the essence of the historic landmark. As they approached the cake, Caleb and Meghan couldn't help but marvel at its beauty. It was a fitting tribute to their wedding venue and a symbol of their love story, set against the backdrop of Transylvania's rich history.

The guests cheered as Caleb and Meghan cut the cake together, symbolizing the sweetness and unity of their bond. The reception was filled with laughter, music, and the clinking of glasses as they celebrated their love and the start of their new journey together as husband and wife. The aroma of delicious food, the sight of the stunning cake, and the love in the room created a magical atmosphere that Caleb and Meghan would cherish for a lifetime.

After enjoying a delicious feast of traditional Romanian delicacies and savoring every bite of the Bran Castle-themed wedding cake, Caleb and Meghan were ready for the next special moment of the evening. As the music swelled and filled the room, Caleb and Meghan took to the dance floor for their first dance as husband and wife. The romantic melody enveloped them, and they moved together in perfect harmony, their gazed locked on each other with love and adoration.

In that moment, surrounded by the historic walls of Bran Castle, Caleb and Meghan danced as if they were the only two people in the world. Each step, each twirl, was a symbol of their unity and the promise they made to each other. Their dance was a beautiful expression of their love, a celebration of their journey together and the beginning of a new chapter in their lives. As they moved together, lost in the music and the moment, Caleb and Meghan knew that their love was stronger than ever and that their future was filled with endless possibilities.

The guests watched in awe, their hearts touched by the love and connection that Caleb and Meghan shared. It was a moment of pure magic, a memory that would forever be etched in their hearts as the beginning of their happily ever after.

As the evening drew to a close and the celebrations of Caleb and Meghan's wedding came to an end, the photographer approached them with two large envelopes in hand. The envelopes were filled with all the photos that were taken throughout the day, capturing every moment of their special day in stunning detail. With a warm smile, the photographer handed the envelopes to Caleb, who accepted them with gratitude and excitement. The envelopes were heavy with memories, each photograph holding a piece of their love story and the joy of their wedding day.

Caleb and Meghan couldn't wait to relive each moment, from the tender exchange of vows to the joyous celebration with the Transylvanian locals. The photographs would serve as a timeless reminder of the love they shared, the promises they made, and the beginning of their journey as husband and wife.

As they bid farewell to their guests and prepared to leave Bran Castle, Caleb held the envelopes close to his heart, knowing that these photos would be cherished for a lifetime. With a final glance back at the castle, Caleb and Meghan walked hand in hand into the night, ready to start their new life together.

Before they had gotten too far, a group of Romanian ladies approached them, speaking in rapid, fluent Romanian. The ladies were beaming with joy and excitement, their eyes alight with warmth as they presented Caleb and Meghan with a beautifully handcrafted quilt. The quilt was a work of art, filled with intricate designs and vibrant colors that told a story of tradition, love, and craftsmanship. It was a heartfelt gift from the local women, a symbol of their blessings and well-wishes for the newlyweds.

In awe and gratitude, Caleb and Meghan accepted the quilt, their hearts touched by the generosity and thoughtfulness of the gesture. Caleb, who spoke fluent Romanian, expressed his thanks to the ladies in their native language, his words filled with sincerity and appreciation.

"Va multumesc din suflet pentru acest dar minunat," Caleb said, his voice filled with emotion. "Suntem profund recunoscatori pentru gestul vostru frumos. Va multumesc!"

The Romanian ladies smiled warmly at Caleb's words, their eyes twinkling with happiness at his appreciation. They nodded in acknowledgement, their hands clasped together in a gesture of goodwill and friendship.

With the handmade wedding quilt in hand and the memories of their special day etched in their hearts, Caleb and Meghan bid farewell to the ladies and continued on their journey, their hearts full of gratitude for the love and kindness they had received on their wedding day. The quilt would serve as a treasured reminder of the warmth and generosity of the Romanian people, a symbol of the love and blessings that surrounded them on their magical day.

With the wedding quilt in hand and their hearts filled with love and joy, Caleb led Meghan to a secluded spot at the edge of the city. The night was still young, the sky above them twinkling with stars, reflecting the happiness in their hearts. Once they were away from prying eyes, Caleb took a deep breath and turned to face Meghan. His eyes sparkled with a mixture of excitement and love as he gently took her hand. In an instant, a warm, glowing light enveloped them, teleporting them from edge of the city to the comfort of their spacecraft. The transition was smooth and swift, a testament to the advanced technology of their spacecraft.

As they reappeared in their spacecraft, they were greeted by the familiar hum of the engines and the soft, comforting glow of the interior lights. They had returned home, their hearts brimming with love and their minds filled with memories of their wedding day. In the tranquility of their spacecraft, far above the earth, Caleb and Meghan held each other close, the wedding quilt wrapped around them like a warm embrace. They gazed out at the stars, their hearts united in love and their future as limitless as the universe that surrounded them.

Before Meghan could even register what was happening, Caleb swept her off her feet, his arms cradling her in a loving embrace. With a spark in his eyes and a playful smile on his lips, he carried her into the bedroom, their laughter echoing through the spacecraft.

The bedroom was a cozy and intimate space, filled with personal touches that made it feel like home. One of those touches being a special place in the closet that Caleb had prepared for their wedding clothes. It was a thoughtful gesture that made Meghan's heart flutter with love and appreciation.

Caleb gently set Meghan down and helped her out of her wedding gown, his hands brushing against the fabric, he looked into her eyes, a question on his lips. "Are you ready for Maldives?" he asked, his voice filled with excitement and anticipation.

The Maldives had been their dream honeymoon destination, a paradise of white sandy beaches, crystal clear waters, and breathtaking sunsets. It was the perfect place for them to relax and enjoy the start of their married life together. Meghan's eye lit up at the mention of the Maldives, a wide smile spreading across her face. She was more than ready to escape to the tropical paradise with Caleb, to make new memories as husband and wife. The thought of spending their honeymoon in such a beautiful place, with the man she loved, filled her heart with joy and anticipation.

Wrapped in Caleb's arms, Meghan nodded, her eyes sparkling with excitement. "I can't wait," she said, her voice filled with happiness. Their wedding day had been perfect, and she knew their honeymoon would be just as magical. She leaned in, giving Caleb a loving kiss, ready to embark on their next adventure together.

Caleb, with a soft smile still adorning his face from Meghan's reaction, carefully undid his suit. He pulled off his jacket, then his waistcoat, followed by his tie and shirt, before finally stepping out of his trousers. Caleb carefully hung their wedding attire in the dedicated space. The sight of their wedding clothes, hanging side by side in the closet, was a heartwarming reminder of their vows and the beautiful day they had shared.

With their wedding clothes safely stored away, Caleb pulled Meghan into his arms, holding her close. Their eyes locked, and in that moment, they both knew that they were exactly where they were meant to be – with each other, in each other's arms. Her lips met his in a sweet, lingering kiss, expressing her love and appreciation for him. As their lips parted, Meghan rested her head against his chest, listening to the steady rhythm of his heartbeat.

"I need to go set the GPS, I will be right back," Caleb said, as he slipped on a pair of comfortable shorts and made his way to the navigation system room. With a few deft movements, he programmed the spacecraft's GPS for their next destination – the Maldives. The anticipation of their honeymoon added an extra spring to his step as he returned to the bedroom.

As he walked back into the room, he noticed a change. Meghan had put on one of Caleb's t-shirts. The oversized garment cascaded over her petite frame, making her look even more endearing. A soft smile played on his lips at the sight of her, a familiar warmth spreading in his chest.

"Meghan," he called out softly, his tone filled with affection. "You look beautiful." His words were simple, yet sincere. Despite the change of clothes, or perhaps because of it, he found her even more attractive. It was one of those small, intimate moments that made him realize how deeply he was in love with her, and how excited he was to start this new chapter of their life.

With her eyes sparkling and a smile playing on her lips, Meghan gave a playful twirl in Caleb's t-shirt. The soft fabric billowed around her as she spun, adding a whimsical charm to the moment. Her laughter echoed in the room, a beautiful melody that made Caleb's heart flutter.

After her playful twirl, Meghan made her way towards the bed. She crawled under the covers, her eyes still shining with happiness and love. She looked up at Caleb, her gaze inviting him to join her. Caleb couldn't help but smile at Meghan's antics. He loved her playful side, just as much as he loved every other facet of her personality. With a soft chuckle, he moved towards the bed, ready to join his wife for their first night together as a married couple.

As Caleb slipped into bed next to Meghan, she welcomed him with a warm smile. As he reached out, her fingers lightly tracing a path down Caleb's chest. Her touch was gentle, yet filled with love, a silent expression of her deep feelings for him. Caleb watched her, his heart swelling with love and affection. He reached out, capturing her hand and bringing it to his lips. He planted a soft kiss on her fingers, his eyes never leaving hers.

The day had been long and filled with joyous celebrations. Now, in the quiet intimacy of their spacecraft, they found comfort and peace in each other's presence. As they settled down for the night, their hearts intertwined, they looked forward to the adventures that awaited them in the Maldives.

Meghan leaned in, her eyes sparkling with love and affection. Their lips met in a series of tender kisses, each one expressing their deep love for one another. It was the perfect ending to their wedding day and the perfect beginning to their life together as husband and wife. As they lay there, wrapped in each other's arms, their hearts filled with love, they knew they were ready to face whatever the future had in store for them. Together.

With a twinkle in his eyes, Caleb leaned in, capturing Meghan's lips in a passionate kiss. His hand found its way underneath the oversized t-shirt she was wearing, gently tracing the curve of her waist. The softness of her skin against his hand sent a wave of warmth coursing through him.

Their kiss deepened, their hearts beating in sync with each other. It was a moment of pure intimacy, a testament to the deep connection they shared. As they pulled away from the kiss, they shared a soft smile, their eyes shining with love and adoration.

Feeling Caleb's touch, Meghan wrapped her arms around his neck, pulling him closer. Their kiss deepened, igniting a passionate fire within them. Their hearts pounded in their chests, their breaths mingling as they lost themselves in each other. Feeling the heat of their passion, Caleb gently pulled the oversized t-shirt over Meghan's head, breaking their kiss only for a moment.

He tossed the shirt aside, his eyes never leaving Meghan's. His gaze was filled with love and desire, a silent testament to the depth of his feelings for her. In the quiet tranquility of their spacecraft, far above the Earth, they found comfort and love in each other's arms.

In the dim light of their spacecraft's bedroom, Caleb's hands gently slid Meghan's panties off her, his touch causing a shiver of anticipation to run down her spine. Then, he slipped out of his shorts, leaving them both in a state of complete undress.

With the last barriers of clothing gone, they surrendered themselves to each other, their bodies entwining in the dance of love. Their breaths mingled, their hearts pounded in sync, and their bodies moved in perfect harmony, creating a symphony of love and passion.

The rest of the universe faded into insignificance as they lost themselves in each other. Their love transcended the confines of the spacecraft, reaching out to the stars, as limitless and as timeless as the cosmos itself. Their wedding day had been a celebration of their love, and their wedding night was a celebration of their unity. It was a night of passion and intimacy, a night where they truly became one.

Chapter 6

As the first rays of sunlight pierced the sky, the spacecraft, shrouded by the invisibility cloak, hovered silently above the Maldives. The night had been a blur of passion and intimacy, a testament to their deep love for each other.

From their vantage point high above the Earth, they could see the breathtaking beauty of the Maldives. The islands were a spectacular sight, with their white sandy beaches, turquoise waters, and lush greenery. It was a tropical paradise, an idyllic setting for their honeymoon.

As they looked down at the paradise awaiting them, Meghan and Caleb shared a look of excitement and anticipation. Their wedding day had been magical, their wedding night passionate, and now they were ready to create new memories in the beautiful Maldives.

"Caleb," Meghan said, her voice filled with excitement as she looked at the beautiful islands below them. Caleb turned to her, a soft smile playing on his lips. "Meghan," he began, his voice firm but gentle. "I need you to stay here on the spacecraft while I teleport down to secure one of the Maldives islands for us. I want to make sure we have a private and secluded place, just for ourselves."

Meghan looked at him, her eyes wide with surprise. "You can do that?" she asked, her voice filled with awe. Caleb chuckled, nodding his head. "Yes, love. I can do that." With a reassuring squeeze of Meghan's hand, Caleb disappeared, teleporting down to the islands below. His mission was to secure a perfect, secluded spot where they could enjoy their honeymoon in peace and privacy.

Left alone in the spacecraft, Meghan eagerly awaited Caleb's return, her heart filled with anticipation for the adventures that awaited them on their private island in the Maldives. Appearing on one of the beautiful islands of the Maldives, Caleb quickly set his plan into motion. He had a particular island, renowned for its pristine beaches and untouched beauty.

Finding a local man, he greeted him with a respectful nod before switching to Dhivehi, the local language of the Maldives. The man looked surprised but pleased at Caleb's fluency, a smile spreading across his face.

"Kihineh Virgin Island eh beynunvanee?" Caleb asked, inquiring about the price of the Virgin Island. The man's eyes widened in surprise, clearly not expecting such a question. Caleb waited patiently for the man's response, ready to negotiate if necessary. He was determined to secure the Island for their honeymoon, wanting to give Meghan the most unforgettable experience. Little did he know, their adventure in the Maldives was just beginning.

The man, taken aback by Caleb's question, quickly regained his composure. He gave Caleb a thoughtful look before responding in Dhivehi. "Miadhu, koba dheynan tha? Virgin Island, eh hoadhaanee ehgothah Maldive Island Properties ga," he said, giving Caleb directions to the Maldives Island Properties, a local real estate agency that handled such transactions.

Caleb thanked the man and made his way towards the agency. He was focused, ready to do whatever it took to secure the Virgin Island for their honeymoon. As he walked, he couldn't help but feel a rush of excitement. He was about to purchase an Island in one of the most beautiful places on Earth, all for Meghan and their honeymoon. He could hardly wait to see Meghan's reaction when she found out about the surprise he had in store for her.

Upon stepping into the agency, Caleb was met with a professional atmosphere and a woman seated behind a sleek desk. As he confidently greeted her in Dhivehi, her eyes widened in surprise. "Assalaamu Alaikum. Mee Caleb ah," he introduced himself, his fluency in Dhivehi impeccable. "Mihaaru Virgin Island eh beynunvaa. Baeh naganee."

Taken aback by his request, the woman blinked in surprise. It wasn't every day someone strolled into her office to purchase an entire island, especially not the Virgin Island. Regaining her composure, she returned to her professional demeanor. "Mr. Caleb, miadhu koba Virgin Island eh beynunee ehgothah check kuranee," she responded in Dhivehi, indicating she would check the availability and process for purchasing the Virgin Island.

As she turned to her computer, Caleb leaned back in his chair, a satisfied smile on his face. He was eager to see Meghan's reaction upon learning he had purchased an entire island for their honeymoon.

After a few moments of checking, the lady turned back to Caleb. She wore a professional smile, her eyes meeting his. "Mr. Caleb," she began in Dhivehi. "Virgin Island eh beynunee ah 50 million dollars." She paused for a moment, gauging his reaction. It was a hefty sum, even for an island as beautiful and untouched as the Virgin Island. But Caleb didn't bat an eyelid. Price was not an issue for him. His only concern was giving Meghan a perfect honeymoon.

With a nod of his head, he accepted the price. He was ready to finalize the deal and secure the island for their honeymoon. Caleb did not hesitate. He pulled out his credit card, completing the transaction swiftly. $50 million was a small price to pay for the happiness of the woman he loved.

"Shukuriyyaa," he said to the lady, thanking her in Dhivehi. His eyes were bright with excitement, the thought of surprising Meghan with an entire island making his heart race. With the deal finalized and the Island now theirs, Caleb couldn't wait to return to Meghan and tell her the good news. He knew she was going to be thrilled. After all, a private island in the Maldives was a dream come true for anyone, let alone for a honeymoon.

When Caleb teleported back to the spacecraft, he found Meghan curled up on the couch, fast asleep. He paused for a moment, drinking in the sight of her. Her chest rose and fell gently with each breath, her face peaceful in sleep. A soft smile tugged at his lips as he watched her, his heart full of love.

This woman, this beautiful earthling, was now his wife. She had accepted him, loved him unconditionally, not caring that he was from another galaxy. She had embraced him with all his differences, all his uniqueness. And now they were on this incredible journey together, about to start their life as a married couple on an island in the Maldives.

Caleb's smiled widened as he looked at Meghan. He was the luckiest man in the universe, and he couldn't wait for her to wake up, her dream honeymoon would become a reality. Quietly, so as not to disturb Meghan's peaceful slumber, Caleb made his way to the navigation room of the spacecraft. He sat down in front of the controls, his fingers dancing over the buttons and switches with practiced ease.

His first task was to set the coordinates for the Virgin Island. He could still hardly believe it – he had bought an entire island for their honeymoon. The thought brought a smile to his face. He couldn't wait to see Meghan's reaction.

With everything set, Caleb initiated the descent. The spacecraft, invisible to the world, began its gentle descent towards the Virgin Island. Their honeymoon adventure was about to truly begin, and Caleb couldn't be more excited.

The spacecraft touched down gently on the Virgin Island, the soft hum of the engines slowly fading away as the vessel settled on the sandy beach. The slight jolt of the landing stirred Meghan from her sleep. With a soft yawn, she sat up on the couch, rubbing her eyes. The unfamiliar surroundings took her a moment to register before she remembered where she was.

"Caleb?" she called out, her voice soft and slightly groggy. From the navigation room, Caleb heard Meghan's call. A smile touched his lips as he rose from his seat. "I'm here, love," he responded, making his way back to her.

As Caleb sat down next to Meghan on the couch, he turned to her with a soft smile on his face as he took her hands in his. "Honey," he began, his voice filled with excitement. "I bought an entire island for our honeymoon. It's called Virgin Island and it's all ours. You can even change the name if you want."

He watched her face, eager to see her reaction. This was a big surprise, and he could hardly wait to see her response. Despite his otherworldly abilities, it was these human moments, these expressions of love and joy, that he cherished the most. Meghan, his earthling wife, had taught him that.

Meghan's eyes widened in surprise, a smile spreading across her face. "You're joking, right?! An entire island? Really?!" she gasped, unable to contain her excitement. Her laughter filled the spacecraft, a joyous sound that made Caleb's heart flutter. In a burst of exuberance, she jumped into his lap, her arms wrapping around in a warm hug. She peppered his face with kisses, her joy infectious.

Caleb laughed, wrapping his arms around her. "I'm not joking, love. The entire Virgin Island is ours," he confirmed, his voice filled with happiness. Her excitement, her joy, her love; it was all worth it. As they sat there, laughing and celebrating, Caleb knew he had made the right decision. Their honeymoon on the Virgin Island was going to be an adventure they'd remember for a lifetime.

Meghan looked at him, her eyes shining with excitement. "Can we go see it right now??" she asked, barely able to contain her eagerness. Caleb chuckled, loving her enthusiasm. "Of course, love. Let's go explore our island," he responded, standing up and helping her to her feet.

With Meghan's hand in his, Caleb led her towards the exit of the spacecraft. As the doors slid open, the sight of the Virgin Island in all its glory came into view. Their adventure was about to begin and Caleb couldn't wait to explore every inch of the island with Meghan. Their honeymoon was going to be unforgettable, a memory they would cherish for the rest of their lives.

As they disembarked from the spacecraft, their feet sinking into the white sandy beach, Meghan gasped. She looked around, her eyes wide with awe at the beauty that surrounded them. The island was breathtakingly beautiful. Pristine, white sand stretched out as far as the eye could see, leading up to the edge of a vast, shimmering ocean. Palm trees swayed gently in the breeze, providing shade and a sense of tranquility. The air was filled with the smell of the sea and the sound of the waves crashing against the shore.

"It's...it's beautiful," Meghan breathed, her hand tightening around Caleb's. "I can't believe this is ours." Caleb looked at her, a smile on his face. Seeing her so happy, so excited, made buying the island worth every penny. He squeezed her hand in return, his eyes filled with love. "Welcome to our island, love," he said, his voice filled with emotion. "Welcome to our paradise."

Meghan turned to Caleb, her eyes sparkling with curiosity. "Is there a place for us to stay?" she asked, looking around the untouched island. Caleb shook his head, his smile never leaving his face. "Not yet, love. But you tell me what you want, and it's yours," he promised, his gaze never leaving her.

He was ready to give Meghan her dream home right here on the island, a sanctuary where they could start their new life together. Whether she wanted a cozy cottage or a grand mansion, he would make it happen. Meghan's smile widened at his words, excitement bubbling within her.

Meghan's eyes sparkled with excitement as she began to describe her dream home. "Like a luxury vacation home with a swimming pool, hot tub, and more," she said, her words filled with enthusiasm. Caleb chuckled, nodding in agreement. "Consider it done, love," he promised. "We'll have the best vacation home right here on our island. It'll be our own little paradise."

With a plan in mind, Caleb could already envision the luxury home. Modern architecture, all glass and steel, blending seamlessly with the natural beauty of the island. A large swimming pool overlooking the ocean, a hot tub under the stars, and all the luxuries they could ever dream of.

With Meghan's dream home clearly pictured in his mind, Caleb raised his hand. He focused on the image, his otherworldly powers bringing it to life. In a swirl of light and energy, the sand beneath their feet began to shift and move. The transformation was swift but spectacular. Before their eyes, a luxury vacation home began to take shape.

The house was stunning. Modern architecture with floor-to-ceiling glass windows, ones that you could see out but not see in, that offered breathtaking views of the ocean. A large, sparkling swimming pool overlooked the beach, and a hot tub was nestled under the shade of a palm tree.

Inside, the house was just as magnificent. Luxurious furnishings, a state-of-the-art kitchen, and a master suite that boasted a panoramic view of their island paradise. As the light faded, Caleb turned to Meghan, a satisfied smile on his face. "Welcome home, love," he said, his voice filled with affection.

Meghan's smile was radiant as she wrapped her arms around Caleb's neck. "How did I ever get so lucky to have someone like you fall in love with me?" she asked, her eyes shining with love and admiration. Caleb looked at her, his heart full of warmth. He brushed a stray strand of hair from her face, his hand gently cupping her cheek. "Meghan, we were destined across dimensions," he replied, his voice soft yet filled with conviction.

And with that, he leaned in to seal his words with a tender kiss, their new home and the beautiful island serving as the backdrop to their perfect moment. As they pulled away from their tender kiss, Meghan wore a beautiful smile. "That will be our first daughter's name," she said, her voice filled with affection, "Destiny Star Stozick."

Caleb's heart swelled at the thought. The idea of starting a family with Meghan, of having a little girl named Destiny, filled him with joy. He loved the name, loved the meaning behind it. It was perfect. He pulled Meghan close, wrapping his arms around her. "Destiny Star Stozick," he repeated, the name rolling off his tongue, "I love it."

In this moment, as they stood in front of their new home on their own private island, Caleb knew they were creating their own destiny.

As they strolled hand in hand along the wooden pathway leading to their new house, Caleb turned to Meghan with a mischievous smile. "I have one more surprise for you, love," he announced, his eyes twinkling with anticipation.

Upon entering their new home, Caleb guided Meghan towards the master suite. It was a grand room with a stunning view of the beach, but what caught Meghan's eye were two large doors on either side of the room.

Caleb gestured towards one of the doors. "This is your closet," he revealed, his voice filled with excitement. As Meghan pushed open the door, her eyes widened in surprise. The walk-in closet was filled with a whole new wardrobe. Beautiful dresses, stylish tops, comfortable loungewear, shoes of all kinds, and accessories to match. It was every fashion lover's dream.

"I know how much you love clothes," Caleb said, watching her reaction. "So, I thought you'd appreciate a new wardrobe for our new life here." Meghan looked at him, her eyes shimmering with happiness. This was more than she had ever dreamed of, and all thanks to Caleb, her loving husband.

Overwhelmed by the thoughtfulness and love of her husband, Meghan felt tears prick her eyes. She quickly moved to wrap her arms around Caleb, burying her face in his chest. "I love you so much, Caleb," she murmured, her voice choked with emotion. "So much so, that there are no words to describe."

Caleb held her close, his own eyes misting over with emotion. He gently stroked her hair, whispering soothing words into her ear. "I love you too, Meghan. More than words can ever express," he replied, his voice filled with love and warmth.

With a small sigh, Meghan pulled back slightly, looking up into Caleb's eyes. Her face was flushed with happiness, her eyes shining with unshed tears of joy. She rose onto her tiptoes, pulling Caleb's head down towards her own. Their lips met in a passionate kiss, a testament to the deep love they shared. It was a promise of a lifetime of happiness and adventures together.

As they pulled away, they remained in each other's arms, their foreheads resting against each other. Words weren't needed in that moment; their feelings for each other were clear in their actions, their expressions.

With a gentle smile, Caleb pulled back from their embrace and looked into Meghan's eyes. "How about we make our first breakfast in our new home?" he proposed, a hint of excitement in his voice. He gestured towards the new state-of-the-art kitchen, complete with modern appliances and a beautiful island counter. It was the perfect place to create delicious meals and memories together.

Meghan's eye lit up at the idea, her earlier tears of joy replaced by a spark of excitement. "I'd love to, Caleb," she agreed, her voice filled with anticipation. Hand in hand, they walked towards their new kitchen, ready to whip up their first meal in their new home.

As they entered the kitchen, Caleb moved towards the large, stainless-steel refrigerator. He pulled the door open with a flourish, revealing a fully stocked interior. Meghan's eyes widened in surprise. The fridge was filled with all kinds of produce, meats, dairy products, and everything they could possibly need. There was even a selection of her favorite fruits and snacks.

"I thought we could use some provisions," Caleb said with a grin, looking at Meghan's stunned expression. "I hope I got everything you like." Meghan looked at him, her surprise turning into a warm smile. "You think of everything, don't you?" she said, her voice filled with affection.

Caleb shrugged modestly, but he couldn't hide the pleased look in his eyes. With everything in place, they were ready to start their new life together on the island. And from the look on Meghan's face, Caleb knew he had made the right decision.

With an inviting smile, Caleb turned towards Meghan. "So, anything special you would like for breakfast?" he asked, his gaze warm and inviting. Whether it was a simple dish like scrambled eggs and toast or something more elaborate like pancakes or a full English breakfast, Caleb was ready to whip up anything Meghan desired. After all, this was their first breakfast together in their new home, and he wanted it to be perfect.

Meghan looked momentarily surprised but then returned his smile. "I think some scrambled eggs and toast would be perfect," she replied. "Scrambled eggs and toast, coming right up," Caleb responded, his tone light and cheerful. He moved towards the fridge, ready to prepare their first meal of the day in their new home on their own private island.

With a sweet smile, Meghan offered her assistance. "I'll help by making the toast," she chimed in. Caleb looked over at her and nodded, appreciating her initiative. Together, they moved around the kitchen in a harmonious dance, preparing their breakfast.

Once breakfast was ready, Caleb and Meghan took their places at the table, their plates brimming with scrambled eggs and perfectly toasted bread. The morning sun streamed in through the windows, casting a warm and inviting glow over the room.

As they began to eat, their conversation flowed naturally. They talked about their beautiful island home in the Maldives, discussing their favorite spots and sharing their thoughts on how they could make it even more homely.

They also started dreaming about their next adventure. From exploring the romantic streets of Paris to trekking in the rugged landscapes of Patagonia, they considered all the exciting possibilities. Their shared love for travel was evident in their animated discussion, their eyes shining with excitement and wanderlust.

This breakfast was more than just a meal. It was a moment of connection, a time for them to share and plan their dreams. And as they sat there, in their lovely island home, they felt a deep sense of contentment and joy. They were not just sharing a meal, but also sharing their hopes and dreams, and that made the moment incredibly special.

Once they had finished their breakfast and cleaned everything up, Caleb turned to Meghan with a warm smile. "Would you like to take a walk on 'our' beach?" he asked. Meghan's eyes lit up at the suggestion and she returned his smile with enthusiasm. "I would love to," she replied, eager to enjoy the natural beauty of their island home.

Hand in hand, they left the house and strolled towards the beach, the sound of the waves and the feel of the warm sand beneath their feet adding to the tranquility of the moment. This was their paradise, their sanctuary, and they cherished every moment spent in it.

The sight of the endless ocean surrounding their private island was indeed breathtaking. Azure waves lapped gently at the sandy shores, reflecting the brilliant sunlight. A light breeze carried the scent of salt and sea, adding to the serenity of the scene.

As they walked hand in hand, Meghan found her thoughts drifting towards Caleb's powers. She had always been fascinated by his abilities, but she couldn't help but wonder about the true extent of his capabilities. Could he manipulate the elements at will? Could he conjure up anything he desired? Or were there limitations that he hadn't disclosed?

Despite her curiosity, Meghan felt a sense of comfort knowing that Caleb was always there to protect and care for her. His powers were a part of him, and she accepted them as she accepted him – with love and understanding. As they continued their walk along the beach, Meghan found herself looking forward to discovering more about Caleb and the magical world they shared.

Caleb, noticing Meghan's thoughtful silence, gently squeezed her hand and turned to her. His gaze was filled with concern as he asked, "Is everything alright, Meghan?" His warmth and concern brought Meghan back from her thoughts. She gave him a reassuring smile, appreciating his caring nature.

Meghan looked up at Caleb with a glowing smile. "Yes, everything is wonderful," she said, her eyes sparkling with sincerity. Then, with a soft blush tinting her cheeks, she added, "Especially you." The love in her words was unmistakable, a testament to the deep connection they shared.

Their days on the island were a blissful mix of joy, laughter, and love. They spent time cooking meals together, their kitchen filled with the aroma of delicious food and the sounds of their shared laughter. They experimented with new recipes, playfully teasing each other as they cooked.

Their love for each other was evident in every shared glance, every touch, and every word. The passion between them was palpable, filling their island home with a warmth that was far more comforting than the tropical sun.

The time they spent making love was a testament to their deep connection and shared passion. Their love was not just physical, but emotional and spiritual, a bond that was strengthened with each passing day.

Living on the island, away from the rest of the world, allowed them to focus on each other completely. It was their own private paradise, a place where their love could flourish without any distractions or interruptions. And those moments of shared joy and love, they found their own version of paradise.

As the days turned into weeks, and the weeks into months, Caleb and Meghan continued to revel in their island paradise. The change of seasons brought a new beauty to their surroundings. The arrival of spring in April turned their island into a vibrant canvas of colors. The trees were adorned with bright, new leaves, and the air was filled with the sweet scent of blooming flowers. The island was alive with the sounds of birds chirping and the gentle rustle of leaves.

The change of season did nothing to dampen their spirits. Instead, it brought a fresh wave of excitement and anticipation. They spent their days exploring new paths, swimming in the clear ocean, and simply enjoying each other's company. Their island home had given them a unique opportunity to connect with nature and with each other. And as they watched the arrival of spring from their private beach, they couldn't help but feel grateful for the incredible journey they had embarked on together.

During one particular breakfast, as the morning sun streamed in through the windows, Caleb brought up a new topic. "Meghan, do you remember mentioning that you've always wanted to see Egypt?" he asked, his eyes sparkling with a sense of adventure.

Meghan looked up at him, a surprised smile spreading across her face as she recalled the conversation. Egypt, with its ancient history and iconic landmarks, had always been on her list of places to visit. The thought of experiencing it with Caleb added to the excitement. She felt a rush of anticipation as this new adventure they were about to embark on.

Meghan's eyes widened in delight as she absorbed Caleb's words. A smile spread across her face, lighting up her features. "Really? You would take me to Egypt?!" she exclaimed; the excitement clear in her voice.

The prospect of visiting the land of the pharaohs, seeing the pyramids and the Sphinx, exploring the Nile, and immersing herself in the rich history and culture of Egypt was a dream come true for her. The fact that she would be experiencing it all with Caleb made it even more special.

Caleb laughed, his eyes twinkling with amusement at her excitement. "I can take you anywhere you want to go," he assured her, his voice filled with affection. His words were not just a promise of travel, but a testament to his willingness to do anything to make her happy. It was a declaration of his love for her, and it made Meghan's heart flutter with joy. The thought of exploring the world with Caleb by her side filled her with anticipation and delight.

"Whenever you're ready to go to Egypt, just let me know," Caleb told her, his voice filled with excitement at the prospect of their next adventure. Meghan, however, looked slightly worried. "But what about our things here? Will they be safe?" she asked.

Caleb gave her a reassuring smile. "Don't worry, Meghan. Our island, and everything on it, will be under an invisibility cloak," he explained. "No one will be able to see or access it while we're gone." The relief on Meghan's face was palpable. She trusted Caleb, and knowing that their home would be safe in their absence brought her a sense of peace. She was ready to embark on this new adventure, to explore the wonders of Egypt with the man she loved.

A warm smile spread across Meghan's face as she took Caleb's hand in hers. "Caleb," she started, her voice filled with emotion. "I need you to know how much I love and adore you." Her words were heartfelt and sincere, a testament to the deep bond they shared. She looked into his eyes, letting him see the depth of her feelings for him. It was a moment of pure love and vulnerability, a moment that further strengthened their connection.

Caleb looked back into Meghan's eyes, his own reflecting the love he felt for her. "Meghan, I feel the same about you," he confessed, his voice low and full of emotion. His words echoed in the quiet room, a profound declaration that filled their hearts with warmth and happiness. The bond between them was undeniable, a love that was as deep and vast as the ocean surrounding their island.

As Caleb activated his teleportation device, they were enveloped in a soft light before finding themselves aboard his spacecraft. Meghan looked around, still in awe of the advanced technology surrounding them.

"Caleb, can I sit with you in the observation deck while you set up navigation to Egypt?" she asked, her eyes shining with curiosity and excitement. Calebsmiled at her enthusiasm, his heart swelling with affection. "Of course, Meghan," he replied, taking her hand and leading her towards the observation deck. Their new adventure was about to begin, and they were ready to face it together.

As they reached the observation deck, Meghan gazed down at where their island home should have been. But there was nothing. The ocean was a vast expanse of blue, uninterrupted and serene. "Wow, you weren't kidding," she gasped in awe. "The whole island is hidden, like it's not even there!"

Caleb simply smiled, a hint of pride in his eyes. "Told you," he said, taking a moment to appreciate the marvel of his technology. Caleb watched Meghan, her face lit up with excitement and awe, and he couldn't help but feel a sense of joy. Her enthusiasm was infectious, reminding him of a child on Christmas morning – pure, unrestrained, and full of wonder.

Her excitement brought a freshness to his world, a spark that made even the most mundane things seem extraordinary. It was the way she embraced life, with open arms and a thirst for knowledge, that made him fall for her even more with each passing day.

Watching her, Caleb felt a warmth spread through his chest. How lucky he was, he thought, to have found someone who could appreciate the world as much as he did, someone who could find joy in the simplest of things. He couldn't wait to share more of his world with her.

Meghan turned to Caleb, a curious smile on her face. "So, how long before we get to Egypt?" she asked. Caleb grinned back at her. "Well, we could get there instantly," he said, his eyes twinkling with mischief. "But that would take the fun out of traveling, wouldn't it?"

He knew they could teleport straight to Egypt, but he also knew that the journey was half the adventure. Traveling through space, witnessing the wonders of the universe, and experiencing it all with Meghan by his side was something he wouldn't trade for anything.

"Besides," he continued, "I think you'll enjoy the ride." His smile widened as he began setting up navigation, looking forward to the journey ahead. Meghan looked at Caleb with a mischievous smile, her eyes sparkling with anticipation. "As long as I'm with you, I know I will enjoy it," she declared confidently.

Her words filled Caleb with warmth, his heart beating a little faster at her declaration. He knew they were about to embark on an adventure of a lifetime, and he was glad that he would be able to share it with Meghan. With a soft smile, Caleb reached out and squeezed Meghan's hand reassuringly, ready to embark on their journey to Egypt.

With the navigation system set for Egypt, Caleb turned to Meghan. "Ready to relax?" he asked, offering her a warm smile. Meghan nodded, returning his smile. "Absolutely," she replied.

Hand in hand, they made their way to the living area as comfortable and homely as possible, knowing how important it was to have a space to unwind and relax during their travels.

They settled into the soft couch, turning on the TV to watch their favorite shows as they journeyed towards Egypt. It was a simple moment, but it was their moment – a testament to the comfort and love they found in each other's company.

The next few days passed quickly as the spacecraft journeyed towards Egypt. Meghan and Caleb spent their time talking about the sights they were excited to see – the pyramids of Giza, the Sphinx, the bustling markets of Cairo, and the historical treasures in the Egyptian Museum.

They discussed their plans for visiting the Valley of the Kings and Queens, where they would explore the tombs of the ancient Pharaohs. Meghan was particularly excited about seeing the tomb of Tutankhamun, while Caleb was eager to see the temples of Luxor and Kamak.

Their conversations were filled with excitement and anticipation, their shared enthusiasm for the upcoming adventure making the journey pass quickly. They took turns cooking meals, watching movies, and playing games, their comfortable companionship filling the spacecraft with warmth and laughter.

Before they knew it, the spacecraft's navigation system alerted them that they were nearing their destination. The prospect of setting foot in Egypt, a land so rich in history and culture, brought a new surge of excitement. They couldn't wait to start exploring.

Caleb made his way to the observation deck, his eyes scanning the view in front of him. From this height, he could see the dazzling beauty of Egypt spread out below him. The sprawling cities, the vast desert, and the glittering Nile all came together to create a breathtaking panorama.

He knew he needed to find a secluded place to land their spacecraft. A place that was out of sight from the public, yet close enough to the areas they wanted to explore. His eyes scanned the landscape, looking for suitable locations.

After a while, he spotted a secluded area on the outskirts of a desert, a safe distance from the bustling cities and the famous landmarks. It was the perfect spot – hidden from prying eyes, yet accessible enough for them to start their exploration.

With a satisfied nod, he programmed the coordinates into the navigation system. Their Egyptian adventure was about to begin.

"Meghan," Caleb called out, his voice echoing through the spacecraft. "Come to the observation deck. You've got to see this."

Within moments, Meghan appeared at the entrance of the deck, her eyes lighting up at the sight that greeted her. From this vantage point, they could see the entirety of Egypt spread out beneath them, a beautiful tapestry of history and culture.

"Oh, Caleb," she breathed, her hand instinctively finding his as she took in the view. "It's even more beautiful than I imagined. Caleb squeezed her hand, his gaze never leaving the scene below. "And this is just the beginning," he said, excitement threading through his voice. "Just wait until we're on the ground, exploring everything up close.

With their hands intertwined and the beauty of Egypt unfolding beneath them, they stood on the brink of their new adventure, ready to dive in.

Chapter 7

The next morning, as the first rays of sunlight streamed through the window of the spacecraft, Caleb pulled Meghan close to him. He gazed into her eyes, excitement and anticipation reflecting in his own. "Meghan," he said, his voice a soft murmur in the quiet of the morning, "are you ready to go explore Egypt?"

Meghan's eyes sparkled with excitement, her smile matching his own. "I've been ready since the moment we decided to come here," she replied, her voice filled with eagerness. With a shared look of anticipation, they prepared to embark on their Egyptian adventure, ready to discover the secrets and wonders of this ancient land.

"Before we go exploring, how about we have breakfast in Cairo?" Caleb asked Meghan before they stepped out of the spacecraft. His eyes twinkled with anticipation at the thought of their first meal on Egyptian soil.

Meghan's smile widened at his suggestion; her excitement palpable. "Absolutely," she responded, her eyes alight with joy. "I can't wait to hear you speak Egyptian Arabic."

Caleb couldn't help but chuckle, his heart swelling with affection for Meghan's eagerness. His linguistic skills were second to none, fluently speaking every language, including Egyptian Arabic. "Get ready to be impressed," he teased, his eyes sparkling with amusement. He was excited to show off his language skills, and even more so to experience Egypt with Meghan by his side.

Caleb turned to Meghan, a smile playing on his lips. "I did some research last night on places to eat in Cairo," he began, his excitement. "I found this place called Tayer Ya Fatayer Zamalek. It's supposed to have some of the best local cuisine."

Meghan's eyes lit up at his words, her excitement matching his own. She loved trying new cuisines, and the thought of sampling authentic Egyptian food made her stomach rumble in anticipation. "That sounds perfect," she replied, her smile wide. "I can't wait to try it out."

With a shared look of anticipation, they set off towards Cairo, eager to start their culinary adventure in Egypt. With a firm grip on Meghan's hand and a clear mental image of their destination, Caleb activated his teleportation ability. In an instant, they were enveloped in a soft, warm light, the interior of the spacecraft disappearing around them.

When the light faded, they found themselves standing outside Tayer Ya Fatayer Zamalek. The bustling streets of Cairo surrounded them, the vibrant energy of the city a stark contrast to the tranquility of their spacecraft.

Meghan looked around in awe, her eyes wide with excitement. Caleb grinned back at her, his heart swelling with pride. "Welcome to Cairo," he said, gesturing towards the restaurant. "Now, let's get some breakfast."

Caleb reached out, holding the door open for Meghan as they entered Tayer Ya Fatayer Zamalek. The restaurant was bustling, filled with the aroma of fresh bread and spices, the air filled with the murmur of conversation in a mix of languages.

They were seated quickly, a friendly waiter leading them to a cozy table by the window. The waiter handed them two menus, the pages filled with a variety of local dishes. Their adventure in Cairo had officially begun, and they couldn't wait to dive into the Egyptian culinary scene.

As Meghan closed her menu, Caleb caught her eye and gave her a warm smile. "Would you like me to order for us?" he asked, his fingers lightly tracing the edge of his own menu. Meghan returned his smile, nodding in agreement. She loved surprises and she trusted Caleb's judgement when it came to food. "Yes, please. I can't wait to see what you choose," she replied, her eyes sparkling with anticipation.

Caleb chuckled, feeling a spark of excitement himself. He loved introducing Meghan to new experiences and today was turning out to be a perfect day for that. He signaled a waiter and started ordering, his fluent Egyptian Arabic flowing smoothly as he requested a platter for two for their breakfast.

Speaking in fluent Egyptian Arabic, Caleb caught the waiter's attention.

"ثً صخعمي مهنث فاثُنَخطس حمشففثق شي فصخ ةهرثقشم صشفثقسو حمثشسثز"

he ordered, which translated to, "We would like the Ezzo's platter and two mineral waters, please."

The waiter nodded in understanding, quickly scribbling down their order before disappearing into the kitchen. Turning back to Meghan with a twinkle in his eye, he said, "I think you're going to enjoy the Ezzo's platter.

Meghan grinned back at him; her enthusiasm infectious. This was one of many experiences she was looking forward to in Cairo. Their Egyptian adventure was only just beginning, and she could hardly wait to uncover more of what this ancient city had to offer.

After a few minutes, the waiter returned with their breakfast. The waiter returned, balancing a tray laden with their breakfast. The Ezzo's platter was a feast for the eyes – a medley of traditional Egyptian dishes, each one more tantalizing than the last.

As the waiter set the platter down on their table, the aroma of the fresh, delicately spiced food wafted up to them, making their mouths water. Beside the platter, two glasses of chilled mineral water glistened, the perfect accompaniment to their Egyptian breakfast.

With a nod of appreciation to the waiter, Caleb reached for Meghan's hand, giving it a gentle squeeze. "Ready to dig in?" he asked, his eyes sparkling with anticipation. Meghan inhaled deeply, her eyes closing as she savored the enticing aroma. "It smells wonderful!" she exclaimed, her eyes reopening to meet Caleb's. Her excitement was evident in her wide smile and sparkling eyes.

Caleb grinned at her reaction, equally excited to begin their culinary adventure. "Then let's enjoy our first meal in Cairo," he said, reaching for the serving utensils. As they relished their breakfast, Caleb looked up at Meghan, curiosity dancing in his eyes. "So, what do you want to visit first?" he asked, pausing to take a sip of his mineral water.

Meghan thought for a moment, her eyes gazing out of the window as she considered their options. Cairo was a city rich in history and culture, and there were so many places she wanted to explore. But there was one place that stood out in her mind, a site she'd always dreamed of visiting.

With a grin, she turned back to Caleb, her eyes twinkling with excitement. "How about we start with the Pyramids of Giza?" she suggested, her heart fluttering at the thought of seeing the iconic structures in person.

Once they finished their breakfast, Caleb and Meghan slipped into an alleyway. Caleb took Meghan's hand, their finger intertwining, and in an instant, they were enveloped in a warm, soft light.

When the light faded, they were standing before the Pyramids of Giza. The ancient structures towered over them, an imposing testament to the grandeur and ingenuity of a civilization long past.

Meghan gasped, her hand tightening around Caleb's as she took in the sight. "They're breathtaking," she breathed out, her voice filled with awe. Her eyes were wide as she looked up at the pyramids, her heart pounding in her chest. This was a dream come true, and she couldn't wait to explore the iconic structures up close.

Turning towards Caleb, Meghan wore a bright smile on her face, her eyes reflecting the awe-inspiring view of the pyramids. "Which one should we visit first?" she asked, squeezing his hand excitedly.

Caleb's gaze swept over the three towering structures. They were all equally impressive, each holding its own historical significance. After a moment of consideration, his eyes landed on the largest of the three. "How about we start with the Great Pyramid of Khufu?" he suggested, pointing towards the colossal structure. It was the oldest and most massive of the three, a true wonder of the ancient world.

As they began to approach the Great Pyramid, Caleb turned to Meghan, a serious look on his face. "You know, despite all the exploration and excavation done here, the mummy of Pharaoh Khufu has never been found," he said, his voice filled with a touch of mystery.

Meghan's eyes widened in surprise; her curiosity piqued. "Really?" she asked, her haze shifting between Caleb and the pyramid. The fact added another layer of intrigue to their visit, making the ancient structure even more fascinating.

Before entering the pyramid, Caleb turned to Meghan, a look of concern crossing his face. "Before we go in, I should ask, are you claustrophobic?" he asked, his gaze searching Meghan's.

The interior of the pyramids could be quite confined and he wanted to make sure she would be comfortable. Their adventure was meant to be exciting, but he also wanted to ensure it was a pleasant experience for her.

Meghan smiled warmly at his concern, her hand giving his a reassuring squeeze. "As long as I'm with you, no, I'm not," she replied, her voice steady and confident. A sense of relief washed over Caleb at her words. He returned he smile, his heart swelling with affection. With Meghan by his side, he was ready to explore the mysteries of the ancient pyramid.

As they ascended the worn, ancient steps leading to the entrance of the Pyramid of Khufu, Caleb and Meghan fell silent, awestruck be the view. The vast expanse of the Giza plateau stretched out before them, the golden sand dunes gleaming under the bright Egyptian sun. in the distance, they could see the silhouette of the Sphinx, standing guard over the desert, its enigmatic gaze fixed on the horizon.

Closer, the other two pyramids rose majestically against the clear sky, their stone surfaces weathered by centuries, yet still standing strong. The sight was breathtaking, a stark reminder of the grandeur of an ancient civilization that once flourished on these grounds.

Exchanging a glance, they squeezed each other's hands, their excitement palpable as they stood on the brink of their next adventure.

At the entrance of the pyramid, a slightly narrow tunnel awaited them, leading into the heart of the ancient structure. The stone passageway was dimly lit, creating an atmosphere of mystery and anticipation.

Caleb glanced at Meghan, his eyes seeking assurance. "Ready to enter?" he asked, his voice low yet steady. Despite the initial apprehension, there was an undeniable thrill in his voice, his spirit ignited by the prospect of uncovering the secrets within the pyramid.

Meghan nodded, her grip on his hand tightening. "Let's do this," she replied, determination shining in her eyes. Together, the stepped into the tunnel, leaving the bright Egyptian sun behind as they ventured deeper into the pyramid.

Just a little way in, the tunnel began to slope upwards, transitioning into an uphill walkway. The stone under their feet was worn smooth from centuries of use, and the air grew noticeably cooler as they ascended.

Their footsteps echoed off the ancient stone walls, the only sound in the otherwise silent pyramid. The tunnel was narrow and the ceiling low, but the anticipation of what lay ahead kept them moving forward.

Caleb tightened his hold on Meghan's hand, leading the way as they navigated the incline. They were stepping into a world untouched by time, a place where history whispered in every corner. The thrill of their adventure only grew stronger as they ventured deeper into the heart of the pyramid.

After what felt like an eternity, they finally emerged into the tomb chamber. Despite the long climb, any fatigue they felt was instantly replaced by awe. The chamber was a good size, with high ceilings and intricately carved walls, a testament to the ancient Egyptians' architectural prowess

In the center of the room was the empty tomb, a stark reminder of the pharaoh who once rested here. Despite the absence of Khufu's mummy, the chamber was still filled with an atmosphere of reverence and respect.

Meghan's gaze swept over the room, taking in every detail. "It's hard to imagine that Khufu's body once laid here." She murmured, her voice echoing softly in the chamber. Caleb nodded, his eyes reflecting the same wonder. "It's a piece of history we're standing in," he responded, his hand in hers as they took a moment to appreciate the significance of the place. Even without the remains of the pharaoh, the chamber held a captivating aura of its own, a silent testament to the past.

After a few minutes of absorbing the atmosphere and resting their weary legs, Caleb and Meghan decided it was time to move on. They began their descent, leaving the tomb chamber behind. The journey down seemed shorter; their spirits high from the exhilarating experience.

Once they emerged from the Pyramid of Khufu, the bright Egyptian sun greeted them, a stark contrast to the cool, dimly lit interior they had just left. They paused for a moment, letting their eyes adjust to the light.

Meghan turned to Caleb, a wide smile on her face. "That was incredible," she said, her eyes sparkling with excitement. "Ready for the next?" With a nod and a matching grin, Caleb agreed. "Absolutely. Let's see what the Pyramid of Khafre holds for us." Hand in hand, they set off towards the second pyramid, ready for their next adventure.

As they made their way towards the Pyramid of Khafre, Meghan looked around, her gaze wide in wonder. "This place…it's so amazing," she said, her voice filled with awe. Caleb nodded, a thoughtful expression on his face. "It truly is," he agreed. "But what's even more amazing is what hasn't been discovered yet."

Meghan turned to him, intrigued. "What do you mean?" she asked. "The pyramids are full of secrets," Caleb explained. "There's so much we still don't know about them. Hidden chambers, undiscovered tombs, ancient artifacts…The possibilities are endless."

Meghan's eyes lit up with excitement. The thought of so many secrets still hidden away, waiting to be discovered, only added to the magic of the place. "That's incredible," she breathed out. "It makes you wonder what else might be out there, doesn't it?"

Caleb nodded, his gaze meeting hers. "It certainly does." With that, they continued their journey, their spirits high as they approached the next pyramid, ready to uncover its secrets.

As they neared the entrance to the Pyramid of Khafre, they descended a flight of steps into the heart of the structure. The entrance led to a small tunnel that sloped downwards, adding and air of mystery to their adventure.

Feeling the change in the tunnel's size, Meghan let go of Caleb's hand and instead wrapped her arms around his arm, seeking comfort in his presence. Caleb, noticing the change, stopped in his tracks and turned to her.

"Are you okay, Meghan?" he asked, his eyes filled with concern. He was aware that the tunnel they were in was slightly smaller than the one in Khufu's Pyramid and he wanted to make sure Meghan was comfortable.

Meghan gave him a small nod, squeezing his arm gently. "I'm okay," she assured him. "It's just a bit more...confined than I expected. But I'm alright, really." Caleb gave her a reassuring smile, grateful for her bravery. "We'll take it slow," he promised, and with that, they continued their descent, ready to explore the secrets of the Pyramid of Khafre.

Finally, after what felt like an eternity navigating the narrow, sloping tunnel, they reached the bottom, where the floor leveled out. The space opened up considerably, allowing them to stand up straight once more.

Meghan let out a small sigh of relief, her grip on Caleb's arm loosening. "That's better," she said, managing a small smile as she straightened her back. Caleb chuckled, his own relief mirrored in his eyes. "Exploring these pyramids can really be a workout," he admitted, stretching out his back.

Now that they were in a more open space, they could truly appreciate the interior of the Pyramid of Khafre. The high ceilings and intricate hieroglyphics on the walls made them feel as if they were stepping into another world, one untouched by the passage of time. It was a thrilling, humbling experience, and they couldn't wait to discover more.

As they ventured deeper into the Pyramid of Khafre, the passage once again narrowed into a tunnel. Only this time, it slanted upwards, presenting a new challenge. The dim lighting and close confines could be daunting, but the promise of discovery propelled them forward.

Meghan took a deep breath, her exhale slow and measured. She looked up at the incline, determination flickering in her eyes. "We can do this," she said, her voice steady. Caleb gave her a reassuring squeeze. "We're in this together," he affirmed, his tone echoing her resolve.

With that, they began their ascent, the air growing cooler as they climbed. The silence was broken only by their steady breaths and the quiet scrape of their footsteps against the stone. The sense of anticipation was palpable, the hope of what lay ahead spurring them on.

At the end of the upward slanting tunnel, the path leveled out once more, opening into another passage where they could walk upright. The relief was palpable as they stepped into the more spacious corridor, their bodies grateful for the reprieve.

"I appreciate tall tunnels," Meghan joked lightly, stretching her arms above her head. Caleb laughed, the sound echoing off the stone walls. "You and me both," he agreed, rubbing the back of his neck.

The new tunnel was straight and long, the end lost in the shadows. Hieroglyphics adorned the walls, their ancient stories waiting to be told. The air was cooler here, carrying the scent of ancient stone and dust. The atmosphere was thick with anticipation, every step they took echoing with the promise of discovery.

Arm in arm, Caleb and Meghan continued their exploration, their spirits high despite the physical exertion. The Pyramid of Khafre was proving to be as fascinating as its predecessor, its secrets waiting to be uncovered.

After traversing the long, narrow tunnel, they finally arrived at the tomb chamber where Khafre had once been entombed. The chamber was spacious, its high ceilings adorned with intricate carvings depicting scenes from the pharaoh's life and reign.

In the center of the room stood the empty sarcophagus, a stark reminder of the ancient King who had once rested within. Meghan stepped forward, her gaze fixed on the sarcophagus, "Imagine," she murmured, "Khafre once laid here, surrounded by his riches, his journey to the afterlife guarded by his people."

Caleb joined her, his own eyes filled with awe. "It's a testament to the reverence they had for their leaders," he said. "And a window into a time so different from our own." Though the chamber was devoid of the riches that once filled it, the aura of the ancient past was palpable. They stood in silence, absorbing the atmosphere, their minds filled with images of a civilization that had once been. Their journey through the Pyramid of Khafre had been challenging, but the reward was worth every step.

After a well-deserved rest, Caleb turned to Meghan. "Are you ready to head back?" he asked, his gaze filled with understanding. Meghan let out a sigh, the thought of navigating the narrow tunnels again stirring a hint of apprehension. But she managed a small smile, determined not to let it deter her.

Caleb immediately wrapped his arms around her, pulling her into a comforting embrace. "It's alright, Meghan," he assured her softly, his voice a balm to her worries. "I'm right here with you. We'll take it slow, okay?"

Meghan nodded, her arms wrapping around him in response. "Okay," she murmured, her fears lessening in the face of his support. She took a moment to breathe in his comforting presence, her heart steadying.

With one final look at the tomb chamber, they set off, ready to navigate the tunnels of the Pyramid of Khafre one more time. Together, they would face the challenge, their bond strengthened by the shared experience.

Finally, after a journey filled with wonder and challenge, Caleb and Meghan emerged from the Pyramid of Khafre. The bright Egyptian sun greeted them, the heat a stark contrast to the cool interior they had just left.

Meghan let out a sigh of relief, her shoulders dropping as the weight of their journey lifted. She closed her eyes and tilted her face towards the sun, letting its warmth seep into her skin. "We did it," she said, her voice filled with a mixture of exhaustion and exhilaration.

Caleb nodded, a proud smile on his face. "We did," he agreed, squeezing her hand. "And you were amazing, Meghan."

Their adventure through the pyramids had been a journey of discovery, courage, and shared experience. As they stood there, basking in the warmth of the Egyptian sun, they knew it was an adventure they would never forget.

After a few moments of rest under the warm Egyptian sun, Caleb turned to Meghan, his eyes alight with excitement. "Are you ready to explore the Pyramid of Menkaure?" he asked, his voice filled with anticipation.

Meghan glanced towards the pyramid in question, the smallest of the three, but no less impressive. Despite the fatigue tugging at her muscles, she felt a surge of excitement at the prospect of uncovering more secrets of the ancient world.

She turned back to Caleb, her fatigue replaced with a determined smile. "Let's do it," she said, her voice steady and filled with resolve. They had already conquered two pyramids, and she was ready to face the third. After all, they were in this adventure together, ready to face whatever lay ahead.

With a shared look of excitement and understanding, Caleb and Meghan set off towards the Pyramid of Menkaure, ready to delve into its mysteries.

As they made their way towards the Pyramid of Menkaure, Caleb and Meghan began discussing the history of the pyramids. Caleb and Meghan had a deep interest in history and had done a fair amount of reading about the ancient structures.

They both shared fascinating facts about how the pyramids were built as tombs for the pharaohs and their consorts during the Old and Middle Kingdom periods of Ancient Egypt. They talked about the precision and sophistication involved in creating such grand structures without the aid of modern technology.

Meghan's interest piqued by the rich history, intrigued by the complexities of the ancient civilization and the lasting legacy they had left behind. The stories of the pharaohs who had been laid to rest within the pyramids, their lives, their reigns, and their journeys to the afterlife added a layer of depth to their adventure. As they walked, they found themselves drawn even more into the world of the ancient Egyptians, their anticipation for the next pyramid growing with each step.

As they entered the Pyramid of Menkaure, a wave of relief washed over them. Most of the passages within this pyramid were not as confined as those in the previous two pyramids, allowing them to navigate with greater ease.

Meghan sighed, her breath echoing in the larger space. "I appreciate these wider passages," she said, her voice light with relief. Caleb chuckled, sharing her sentiment. "Yes, it's a nice change," he agreed, looking around at the spacious corridor.

The walls adorned with hieroglyphics and symbols, whispering stories of the past. As the ventured deeper into the pyramid, they found themselves enveloped in an aura of ancient history, their minds buzzing with curiosity and anticipation of the discoveries that awaited them.

As they emerged from the Pyramid of Menkaure, the final pyramid in their exploration, the sun was already dipping below the horizon, casting long shadows across the desert sands. The realization hit them simultaneously - they had been so engrossed in their adventure that they had completely skipped lunch.

Caleb turned to Meghan, a sheepish grin on his face. "I suppose our enthusiasm got the better of us," he said, rubbing the back of his neck. Meghan laughed, her stomach giving an audible grumble. "Definitely," she agreed, her hand resting on her stomach. "I didn't even realize how hungry I was until now."

As they made their way back towards the spacecraft, they laughed at their own forgetfulness. Their shared adventure in the pyramids had been so captivating, they had completely forgotten about their basic needs. But they agreed, it had been more than worth it. Now, however, it was time to remedy their oversight and find a place to satiate their hunger.

Seeing the weariness in Meghan's eyes, Caleb asked her a question. "Do you want to find a place to eat in Cairo or would you prefer going back to the spacecraft to eat. Meghan looked thoughtful for a moment before a slow smile spread across her face. "I think going back to the spacecraft would be best, it has been a long day." she admitted.

As they made their way back to their spacecraft, Caleb couldn't help but feel a sense of contentment wash over him. It had been a long day, full of adventure and discovery, but seeing Meghan so happy made every moment worth it. And he was looking forward to cap the day off with a peaceful meal, just the two of them, under the starlit Egyptian sky.

Caleb gently takes Meghan's hand and led her to a secluded spot, away from prying eyes. He gave her a reassuring smile, his fingers tightening around hers. "Ready?" he asked, his voice soft. Meghan nodded, a sense of anticipation filling her. She had experienced teleportation before, but it never ceased to amaze her.

With a final glance at the Egyptian landscape, Caleb focused on his teleportation abilities and in an instant, they were enveloped by a soft glow, their surroundings blurring before they disappeared. When the light faded, they found themselves back in the familiar interior of their spacecraft. Meghan looked around, a smile playing on her lips.

Caleb released her hand and waved his hand over the table. A full Egyptian meal appeared before them as Meghan watched in awe of Caleb's abilities. Before they sat down, Meghan wrapped her arms around Caleb's neck. "Caleb," she began, her voice barely above a whisper. "I Can't even begin to tell you how much I appreciate all of this. You've taken me to places and shown me things I would never have been able to see without you."

Caleb's heart swelled at her words. He wrapped his arms around her, pulling her closer. "Meghan, you don't know how happy it makes me to share these experiences with you," he confessed, his voice filled with sincerity. Meghan leaned up, planting a soft kiss on his lips. It was a simple gesture, yet it spoke volumes about the deep bond the shared. Their adventures were far from over, and they both looked forward to exploring more of the universe together.

As they sat down to enjoy their meal, their laughter and conversation filling the spacecraft. It was the perfect ending to their day of adventure, a testament to the bond they shared, and the many more adventures to come.

Their conversation naturally drifted back to their adventures within the pyramids. They reminisced about the awe-inspiring hieroglyphics, the grand chambers, and the sheer magnitude of the ancient structures.

Caleb listened intently as Meghan shared her favorite parts of the day, her eyes lit up with excitement. He loved seeing her so animated, her passion for exploration and discovery evident in her words and expressions.

As they finished their meal, they began discussing their plans for the next day. The Great Sphinx of Giza was high on their list, a monument they were both eager to see up close. "I've always been fascinated by the Sphinx," Meghan admitted, her eyes sparkling with anticipation. "Its mysterious allure, the legends surrounding it…I can't wait to see it."

Caleb nodded, sharing her enthusiasm. "It's going to be another day of adventure," he said, his hand reaching across the table to squeeze hers. "And I can't wait to experience it with you."

Their conversation drifted late into the night, the spacecraft humming softly as it hovered above Egypt under an invisibility cloak. As they finally retired, they fell asleep in each other's arms, dreaming of the Sphinx and more Egyptian wonders awaiting them when they awakened the next morning.

The next morning, Caleb was the first to wake. He gently extricated himself from Meghan's embrace, careful not to disturb her. He dressed quietly and made his way to the kitchen. With a wave of his hand, he conjured up a classic breakfast spread – coffee, pancakes, eggs, and bacon. The aroma wafted through the spacecraft, the scent of coffee and bacon particularly potent.

As the delicious smell drifted into the bedroom, Meghan stirred awake. A smile spread across her face as she recognized the familiar aroma. Dressing quickly, she headed to the kitchen. Finding Caleb leaning against the counter sipping his coffee. "Good morning," she murmured. Caleb looked up, his face lighting up at the sight of her. "Good morning," he replied, his voice warm. "Breakfast is ready, my love."

As they sat down to enjoy their breakfast, the promise of another day filled with adventure and discovery lay before them. Their journey to the Sphinx was just hours away. As they savored their breakfast, Caleb looked at Meghan thoughtfully. "How about we do some shopping after we visit the Sphinx?" he suggested. "There are plenty of local markets where we could find some souvenirs."

Meghan's eyes lit up at the prospect. "That sounds like a wonderful idea," she agreed, her excitement palpable. "It would be nice to bring back something tangible to remember our trip."

Caleb nodded, pleased by her reaction. "Great, it's settled then," he said, a warm smile on his face. "We'll visit the Sphinx, then hit the markets."

They finished their breakfast with renewed enthusiasm, discussing what kind of souvenirs they might find. Little did they know, their adventure for the day was only beginning, with the majesty of the Sphinx and the vibrant local markets waiting to be explored.

After finishing their breakfast, Caleb and Meghan were ready to embark on their next adventure to see the Great Sphinx of Giza. Caleb, with a glint of excitement in his eyes, asked Meghan if she was ready to teleport to a secluded spot near the Sphinx.

With a nod from Meghan and a confident smile from Caleb, he focused his energy and in a flash of light, they were whisked away from their spacecraft and appeared in a secluded patch of desert near the Sphinx, away from the bustling crowds of tourists.

Meghan looked around in awe, the Sphinx looming majestically in the distance. The ancient monument exuded an aura of mystery and grandeur. Caleb turned to Meghan, a smile playing on his lips. "Shall we go meet the Sphinx?" he asked, extending his hand to her. Meghan took his hand, her eyes shining with excitement as they made their way towards the iconic monument, ready to uncover its secrets and add another chapter to their shared adventure.

For the next two hours, they found themselves completely engrossed in admiring and exploring the Sphinx. The monumental statue was an awe-inspiring sight up close, its grandeur and intricacy far surpassing what they had imagined.

Caleb and Meghan walked around the monument, their eyes drinking in the majestic sight. They paused frequently to read the information signs posted nearby, each sign providing fascinating insights into the Sphinx's history, construction, and the various legends associated with it.

Meghan sketched the Sphinx in her travel journal, capturing its majestic form and intricate details with her quick, skilled strokes. Caleb watched her, fascination and admiration clear in his eyes. This was another one of their shared moments that he would cherish.

They took their time, savoring the experience and the wealth of information. Their visit to the Sphinx was more than just a sightseeing trip – it was a journey into history, a lesson in architecture, and a testament to mankind's ingenuity. Despite spending the better part of two hours there, they felt that there was still so much to see and learn. But for the day, their time at the Sphinx was coming to an end as they prepared to head to the local markets.

With a final, lingering look at the Sphinx, Caleb teleported himself and Meghan to a secluded spot near one of the bustling local markets. The market was a riot of colors and sounds, with vendors selling everything from jewelry and papyrus scrolls to pottery and textiles.

As they took in their new surroundings, Meghan turned to Caleb with a smile on her face. "Caleb, look at all the small statues of Anubis!" With the mood light and spirits high, they ventured further in the market, ready to explore and find unique souvenirs to take back with them.

As they strolled through the market, Meghan's eyes lit up at the sight of the various trinkets and souvenirs. Every time she really admired something, whether it was a small statue, a piece of jewelry, or a beautifully woven scarf, Caleb made sure to get it for her.

After visiting a few shops, they had accumulated quite a collection of unique items. With a simple wave of his hand, Caleb teleports the bags to the spacecraft, ensuring they didn't have to carry them around.

With their shopping spree successfully concluded, Caleb turned to Meghan. "Are you ready for lunch?" he asked, his stomach growling slightly in anticipation. He had spied a small café that looked very inviting. Meghan nodded, equally excited about the prospect of tasting more of the local cuisine.

Their Egyptian adventure was proving to be more enriching and exhilarating than they had imagined, and they were eager to see what the rest of the day had in store for them.

As they settled down for lunch at a local eatery, the conversation took an unexpected turn. Between bites of delicious falafel and sips of sweet hibiscus tea, Meghan suggested something that made Caleb pause.

"What if we settled down?" she asked, her voice soft yet filled with an unspoken excitement. "You know, get a place of our own." Caleb looked at her, his surprise quickly morphing into curiosity. "Oh? And what kind of place are you thinking?"

Meghan smiled, her eyes distant as she painted a picture with her words. "A ranch," she began. "Somewhere we can have space…away from people. A big, beautiful two-story house with a wrap-around-deck and balconies. A swimming pool with waterfalls and a hot tub for when we want to relax. Lots of animals like horses, cattle, ducks, geese, chickens, and maybe some emus.

Caleb listened intently, his mind filling with images of their dream home. He couldn't help but smile at her enthusiasm. "That sounds incredible, Meghan," he admitted, reaching across the table to squeeze her hand. "Let's start looking as soon as we leave Egypt.

Their conversation continued long after their plates were empty, their hearts filled with dreams of a future home, a place where they could build a life together after their many adventures across the universe.

Chapter 8

As Caleb and Meghan continue their journey to find a place to build their dream life together, they excitedly look for hundreds of acres to purchase for their dream ranch, Luminari Stardust Ranch. After weeks of looking, they finally find a property, 300 acres, 7 ponds, and lots of wooded area with trails.

With a wave of his hand, Caleb sets up the beautiful dream house that Meghan described and everything else needed for the ranch, including a treehouse and swings for their future children.

Everything was, is, and always will be perfect as long as they were together. Meghan wrapped her arms around Caleb's neck, "This is perfect, our own heavenly haven away from the rest of the world.", she said as she looked into his eyes with adoration. Caleb wraps his arms around her waist and kisses her softly on the lips.

A never ending love story that was Destined Across Dimensions.

Made in the USA
Coppell, TX
17 February 2026

71395246R00037